"You do not hunt?"

Sophie's voice almost trembled in amazement.

"No," said Tony. "I am afraid not."

Sophie continued to stare at him.

"Miss Corby," he begged finally, "please do not look at me so. I'm afraid you are quite disappointed in me."

"Not at all!" said Sophie. "I am delighted with you."

"Sophie!" exclaimed her mother and father simultaneously. "You must not regard her, Sir Tony. She is just a child and does not know what she is saying," pleaded Lady Corby with some embarrassment. Sir John was cautioning Sophie to mind her tongue.

Tony had not been prepared for the startling effect of his pronouncement. Grinning at the ease of his success, he said, "Miss Corby, I assure you that you will meet many gentlemen in London who do not hunt."

But as soon as the words were out, he regretted them, for Sophie's eyes lit with hopeful anticipation.

It was then that he decided to enter the chase.

Books by Patricia Wynn

HARLEQUIN REGENCY ROMANCE
THE PARSON'S PLEASURE

Don't miss any of our special offers. Write to us at the
following address for information on our newest releases.

Harlequin Reader Service
901 Fuhrmann Blvd., P.O. Box 1397, Buffalo, NY 14240
Canadian address: P.O. Box 603,
Fort Erie, Ont. L2A 5X3

SOPHIE'S HALLOO

PATRICIA WYNN

Harlequin Books

TORONTO • NEW YORK • LONDON
AMSTERDAM • PARIS • SYDNEY • HAMBURG
STOCKHOLM • ATHENS • TOKYO • MILAN

To my mother

Published October 1989

ISBN 0-373-31112-5

CHAPTER ONE

Sir Desme Orlando Farnham, known by all as Tony, was warming his feet before the fire in his private parlour at the Black Swan. He lay with his shoulders pressed against the back of a sturdy oak chair, his Hessians propped on a low stool, legs crossed at the ankle, hands deeply thrust into his pockets. For many a man this would have been an uncomfortable position. But Sir Tony was lean and limber; it did not disturb him at all. Neither was he overly concerned that this pose might rumple his coat nor spoil his neckcloth, though the cut and quality of both might have adorned the Beau himself.

He yawned contentedly. For the past half-hour he had sat thusly and watched the flaming logs, making little bets with himself about which large splinter of the hot, reddened oak would be the first to succumb and fall amongst the coals below. Now that he was thoroughly warmed, he considered searching out a more lively form of entertainment among the crowd in the public rooms. Perhaps there would be a traveler or a local farmer with whom he could converse. It would please him to hear a country dialect once more before returning to London on the morrow. He had been charmed by the Yorkshire accents he had heard on his recent visit to a friend's country estate.

But the warmth of the hearth and the excellence of the innkeeper's rum punch delayed him, and the coals continued to entertain him, until the sound of raised voices in the passageway offered the possibility of greater amusement. After listening to a rather blustering male voice for a few moments, Tony let his feet drop to the floor and, without taking his hands out of his pockets, launched himself out of the chair with a slight push of his shoulders. He strolled casually to the door that led to the passageway and opened it.

In the hallway, confronting the innkeeper, was a red-faced, bewhiskered gentleman of middle age. He was appropriately dressed for travel, though lacking in the elegance which might distinguish a frequent visitor to Town from a country gentleman. There was a lady standing next to him, presumably his wife, who was pretty, though rather tired and faded. She was quietly and ineffectually making suggestions to her husband. A little ways behind them and off to one side was a young lady—their daughter, Tony guessed. She, unlike her mother, did not seem at all disturbed by the altercation in front of her, but rather was looking about her surroundings in an absent sort of way. She was pretty, too, in a fresh, pleasant fashion, with curling brown hair, brown eyes and features on regular lines.

The girl's mother was still speaking gently, "We can try another inn, dear. There is no need to make a fuss."

But the gentleman would have it not. He ignored his wife's comments and spoke to the innkeeper again, "Come now, my good man. Would you have me believe that there is not one private parlour in this great inn of yours to be had? I tell you, I have traveled enough for one day and I do not wish to go farther. You must have some room."

The harassed innkeeper relented enough to say, "It is as I've told you, sir. I can give your ladies a room together for the night, and I would be willing to turn out my son from his room for *you*, sir, but you will have to take your dinner in the public rooms. All my private ones are taken."

The problem now clear, Tony judged that it was time to intervene. It appeared that his entertainment for the evening had come to him.

"Pardon me," he said. "Perhaps I can be of assistance." Their eyes turned toward him. They had not noticed the fair young man leaning lightly against the doorway with his hands in the pockets of his pantaloons. He lifted himself with another slight push of his shoulder and came forward to greet them with a bow.

"Allow me to introduce myself. I am Sir Tony Farnham. I could not help overhearing your difficulty," he said, smiling, "and I would be honoured if you would share my parlour with me."

The whiskered gentleman looked pleased, but his wife was even more distressed. "Oh, no, sir," she answered quickly. "We could not think of imposing upon your privacy."

But her husband frowned, so Tony responded quickly, "Please. It will be no imposition. I was just thinking how lonely I should be dining with no company."

Before his wife could object again, the gentleman, whose face was taking on a more normal hue, spoke firmly, "Now see there, Clarissa. Let's have no more of that nonsense. Sir," he said to Tony, "we are in your debt. I shall hope to return your hospitality at my club in Town."

"And which club would that be?" asked Tony, ushering them into his snug parlour. He bowed his head politely to the daughter as she followed them through. She seemed no more interested by what was going on now than before and gave him only a perfunctory smile in passing. "Perhaps we are members of the same club?" Tony ended.

The gentleman answered enthusiastically, "Boodles, sir!"

"Ah, yes," Tony said, nodding. "Then you would be Sir John . . . ?"

"Corby, sir!" Sir John answered promptly before giving thought. Then he started with sudden realization. "Did you hear my name mentioned in the passageway?"

"Oh, no," said Tony with a grin. "But you must know it is said that every Sir John in the country belongs to Boodles. I was just playing the odds, but it is rather gratifying to guess right."

Sir John regarded him with less than his previous candour, but there was no malice in Tony's smile, and he relaxed again. "I see. Well then, I take it that you are not a member there."

"No, sir. I am a member of White's. I have lodgings in Arlington Street. Perhaps we shall run into one another in Town."

They were interrupted by the innkeeper who brought them some ale and told them what he could give them for dinner. Tony's speedy resolution of the conflict over rooms had left this hard-pressed man filled with gratitude, for a customer as loud and insistent as Sir John could have disturbed the peace of his house. In a few moments he had left, leaving Tony a mug of ale which was brimming with an especially generous serving.

Sir John resumed where Tony had left off. "We have taken a house in Berkeley Square," he said with a satisfied air. "Perhaps you will call on us there."

"I would be delighted," said Tony. "What part of the country do you come from?"

"From the best county there is!" answered Sir John with conviction.

"And what might that be?" Tony asked politely.

Sir John was astonished, "Why Leicestershire, of course!"

Tony's eyes lit with understanding. "I see. You are a sporting man, Sir John." His guest nodded proudly. "I am surprised to find you on the road at this time of year. I did not think the hunting season was ended up your way."

Sir John's smile faded. He sighed and shook his head. "No, of course not. A couple of fine weeks in March and it's over for you fellows in the plowed countries, but we have another month at least in the grass countries. We are coming to Town because of our daughter, Sophia, here." He turned to look at her resentfully. "Her mother will have it that it is time she was brought out. But," he added philosophically, "she should be married off in no time, and we shall not have to come again until her sister Emma's turn, and that's not for another five years."

"Sir John," Lady Corby scolded gently. "It ought really to be no more than four. As I told you, Sophia ought to have been brought out last year. She is nearly nineteen," she explained to Tony.

Tony smiled at her reassuringly and then turned to Sophia. She had shown no interest in the conversation up until now and still seemed uninspired. Tony thought she must be shy and spoke to her kindly, "One year's difference will not matter in the least. You will find that many girls do not appear until the age of nineteen for various reasons, and no one is the wiser. I congratulate you, Miss Corby, on the prospect of an exciting season.''

The girl looked at him and did not comment. He thought she looked rather wan. Supposing that she did not like to be discussed in this way, he tactfully changed the subject.

''Well, Sir John, let us hope that your stay in London will be a pleasant one. There will be plenty of things in Town to amuse you.'' He raised his glass cheerfully.

But Sir John looked unhopeful. He sighed again. ''I suppose I should be glad that we weren't called upon to come any sooner. I should not have been able to leave before February was out, and I will be worried enough as it is about my youngest hunter, though I gave strict instructions for his care.''

''Oh?'' inquired Tony with the hint of a smile about his lip.

''Yes,'' responded Sir John. ''You see, it was he that I rode on my last hunt just before we left. It was a rare run—over three hours from start to finish. I feared he would not survive it.'' Encouraged by Tony's polite expression, he elaborated, enthusiasm mounting in his voice.

''The fox broke cover just in front of me,'' he began. ''T'was I gave the view-halloo,'' he added modestly, but waited for Tony's congratulations nevertheless before going on. ''Oh, there is nothing in that, I suppose, but you have to have experience to know what to anticipate. Anyway, there I was leading the field on my youngest nag, when what does the villain do but lead the hounds across the fence at its highest point. I was not about to lose the lead so quickly, I assure you, even though it meant putting my horse to a six-rail spot in the fence with two ditches behind. I thought I must certainly lose him on the first go, but he was pluck enough to sail over it without disturbing a rail—just a rather rough landing on the other side. But I stayed seated, and he got to his feet— breathing pretty heavily, of course, but sound on his hooves. After that it was clear running for a while, enough time for him to get his stride, though the pace was rough." Sir John took a sip of his ale as the innkeeper reentered with their dinner. Tony used the interval to seat the ladies at the table and to see that their needs were met.

As soon as they were seated, Sir John continued impatiently, "As I was saying," he said, his fork raised, "my horse had settled in and was going comfortably, still keeping up a spanking pace set by the hounds. (We were not crowding them, mind you—I never try to rush the hounds.) When suddenly, the fox made for a cover the other side of a great ditch. By this time, my hunter was in prime gig and took it sailing with feet to spare."

Tony glanced at the ladies and found that they had silently settled into their meal. Lady Corby was giving her husband her dutiful attention, but there was a fixed look to her features which suggested that she had heard the tale before. Sophia was once again gazing about the room at the furnishings, apparently lost in her own thoughts. Her expression was one of dream-like detachment, which Tony somehow found disturbing. He wondered what she was thinking and what it would take to waken her from her dreamy state. But his family's inattention did not stop Sir John. He gave a full description of the hunt, with each jump, his position in the field, the resulting condition of his horse and the riders who did not survive the ordeal. Tony listened with fascination throughout, but began to wonder after two hours, if the telling of the hunt would duplicate the full three hours of it. Out of the corner of his eye, he could see that Sophia smothered an occasional yawn, while Lady Corby's head was nodding in a highly suspect fashion. Fortunately, however, Sir John wound down.

"And there we were, my youngest hunter and I," he was saying, "having regained the lead after Lord Bixbury's last fall. My horse's sides were heaving so hard that I feared for his survival, I can tell you. When suddenly it all came to an end." He took another swig from his glass. Tony waited expectantly, but Sir John seemed to have come to the end of his tale.

"You caught up with the fox?" asked Tony helpfully.

"No," said Sir John shortly. "The scent was lost. Some scoundrel had let his sheep cross the road at that point, and the hounds were confused. They never did pick up the scent again though we let them search for an hour. And the master of hounds judged it ill-sport to help them along. You've never seen such disappointed animals.''

After two hours, Tony, too, was a bit let down. "Oh," he said lamely, "bad luck." Sir John was staring morosely at the fire, his sympathy for the hounds having overcome him. Tony had to hide an amused grin before turning to the ladies and smiling. This encouragement seemed to work, at least with Lady Corby, who spoke for the first time since the beginning of the meal. "And where do you come from, Sir Anthony?" she asked.

"It is Tony," he corrected her gently. Lady Corby seemed disconcerted by this inconsequence, so he explained. "You see, my name is not Anthony. It is Desme Orlando, after two of my father's friends. My father insisted upon the name even though my mother objected to it strongly. She wanted me to be called Tony, so that is what she called me, and fortunately it stuck—though not with my tutors, naturally." He smiled engagingly, and then seeing comprehension in Lady Corby's eyes, went on to answer her original question.

"I'm from Hampshire."

Sir John roused himself with renewed interest. "Then you must hunt with the Hampshire Hunt," he said. "I've never ridden with them, but Mr. Villebois has bred an exceedingly fine pack. Quite a decorous group, I'm told." He lifted his eyebrows questioningly.

Tony looked at him apologetically. "I'm afraid not," he said.

Sir John was surprised, but not defeated. "Is there a private pack you prefer, then?"

"No," Tony answered with polite regret. "I do not hunt at all."

"You do not hunt?" Tony turned toward Sophia, who had just spoken so incredulously. She was looking at him with eyes opened wide, as though he were the three-legged man at the country fair, and he noticed how large and thickly lashed her eyes were. Sir John was expressing his astonishment in blustering tones, and even Lady Corby looked unsettled.

"No," said Tony again. "I'm afraid not." He looked sincerely regretful, but Sophia continued to stare at him in amazement, and he marvelled that such an insignificant statement could have caused her awakening. "Miss Corby," he begged finally, "please do not look at me so. I'm afraid you are quite disappointed in me."

"Not at all!" said Sophia, wonder in her tone. "I am delighted with you."

"Sophie!" exclaimed her mother and father simultaneously. "You must not regard her, Sir Tony. She is just a child and does not know what she is saying," pleaded Lady Corby with some embarrassment. Sir

John was cautioning Sophie to mind her tongue. But Tony was watching Sophie who, though she blushed at her own words, continued to gaze at him with something like awe and allowed a big smile to spread slowly across her face. As it did so, something extraordinary happened. Two dimples, the deepest Tony had ever seen, marked her peach-coloured cheeks. Her lips parted to reveal two rows of perfectly even white teeth. A gleam of admiration lit her eyes. And the result was an unexpected assault on his senses. He found himself wondering just what it would feel like to rub his own lips gently over those soft cheeks with the dimples, moving ever closer and closer toward those lips.

Something of this inclination must have appeared in his expression, for the girl stopped smiling and regarded him with more reserve. But happily, or so Tony thought it, she did not lose interest again. After eyeing him speculatively for a moment, she asked him, "When you say that you do not hunt, Sir Tony, surely you mean merely that you do not hunt the fox?"

He shook his head solemnly.

"Not hares? Otters? Badgers?" Sophie eyed him sceptically, but after each question, he answered in the negative. "Well," she concluded, almost speechless.

Tony had not been prepared for the startling effect of his pronouncement. Grinning at the ease of his success, he said, "There you go again, Miss Corby. You are looking at me as though I had suddenly sprouted horns. I assure you that you will meet many gentlemen in London who do not hunt." But as soon as he had said so, he regretted it, for Sophie's eyes lit with hopeful anticipation.

"I shall?" she said, almost with a sigh. Tony hoped that he had not lost all competitive advantage with one slip of the tongue.

"Nonsense, girl!" interjected Sir John. "I am sure there is no respectable gentleman who does not hunt—occasionally, at least," he added, qualifying his statement at the sight of Tony's rueful grin. "Of course, there might be some impediment to it. Perhaps you have not had proper introduction to the chase, Sir Tony. You must pay us a call in the Shires. Once you have been blooded and presented with the fox's brush, you will be all set," said he confidently.

"I thank you, Sir John, but I'm afraid nothing can excuse me. I have had ample opportunity to hunt, but find that it does not suit me for several reasons, and, as I am unwilling to devote the proper time to it, have concluded that I had best leave it alone. You will think me a frippery fellow, but I much prefer the amusements of London."

There was nothing inscrutable about Sir John's subsequent expression, but out of politeness to his host, he kept his thoughts to himself. "Well, I do find that queer" was all he said.

"You yourself, I take it, must hunt the majority of your time," said Tony.

"Aye. Six days a week," asserted Sir John.

"It is as I expected," said Tony. "Such devotion does not come cheaply, I'll warrant."

"That it does," agreed Sir John, not without pride. "It takes ten thousand a year just to manage, though last year was a bit worse. I lost three top mounts at £700 each—they each dropped dead with me astride. But this year will be different, I suppose," he added regretfully, remembering his destination.

Tony regarded him with an enigmatic smile. "Just so. You will not need to spend so much in London. And so it is with me," he concluded without explanation. It was getting late, and he wanted to be off early in the morning. He looked at his guests expectantly, but each seemed lost in private thoughts. Sir John was still regretting the rest of the season he would be missing; Lady Corby just looked tired. And Sophie, who had been gazing absently at some remote object, came to when she sensed his eyes upon her. She smiled again, not quite so boldly this time, but questioningly.

Tony took her hand and bowed over it. "I would be honoured if you would allow me to call on you in London, Miss Corby," he said.

Sophie opened her mouth to respond, but her father, suddenly alert, broke her off. "Of course, of course, naturally," he said unconvincingly. "We'll be happy to see you. We must be off to bed now, though, so we can get into Town early tomorrow. I'd better have a word with that innkeeper."

"As to that, Sir John," offered Tony, "it has occurred to me that I have a means of making other ar-
rangements for the night, and I would be happy to give
you my room. No need to wake poor Jem or Dick, as
it is certain to be, and you will have a much better bed.
I shall ask the man to remove my things."

Sir John appeared uncertain, but grudgingly accepted. He had lost much of his enthusiasm for his host
since Tony's admission that he did not hunt, a fact that
did not escape Tony. "If it will not discomfit you too
much," Sir John said with gruff courtesy.

"Not at all," replied Tony. He went in search of the
landlord and gave him his instructions. Then he returned and bade the Corby family good-night. As they
ascended the stairs, Tony was encouraged by the fact
that Sophie looked back at him shyly over her shoulder. Something prompted him to wink at her wickedly
and he was rewarded by seeing her lips form a silent
"o," and then a quick dimple before she turned and
hastened up the stairs.

He looked after her for a moment, grinning speculatively, before returning to the parlour and polishing
off his pint of ale. Then, thrusting his hands once again
deeply into his pockets, he kicked his same oak chair
neatly over to the fire and lowered himself into it. As
he sank lower and lower against the hard back, he lifted
his booted legs, crossed them at the ankle and plunked
them down once again on the footstool.

A tempting thought struck him as he lay there again watching the crumbling coals. What a remarkably fine reward it would be for some lucky fellow to waken such a lovely sleeping beauty as Sophia Corby. He wondered what it would take to make her eyes widen with delight when a man entered the room, and how he could entice those charming dimples more often from their creamy hiding place.

Sophia, he mused sleepily, the wise one. He would find out just how aptly named she had been. Surely there was something out of the ordinary behind that air of vague detachment. Her direct, unschooled manner was intriguing.

Tony smiled as pleasant thoughts and the fire's warmth conspired to make him sleepy, and soon, despite his posture, he dropped easily off to sleep.

CHAPTER TWO

SOPHIE WOKE THE NEXT MORNING feeling much happier than she had expected. She pondered and then remembered the strange gentleman from the night before. At first she had not really noticed him or had dismissed him as being like any other gentleman of her limited acquaintance. But then he had suddenly seemed quite otherwise.

He does not hunt, she thought. The novelty of it was still new and intriguing. She wondered what he could possibly do with his time, and this mystery alone was making her impending trip to London seem less of a misery already.

It was not that Sophie had a disinclination to visit the city of London or even that she was not curious to see it. It was simply that she did not relish the idea of going there to be married off, like a foxhound bitch being sent to be bred. From the little that Sophie had seen of marriage, she had formed a poor impression of it, and she doubted it would please her. But suddenly, it seemed there was a new consideration. Sir Tony had assured her that she would meet many gentlemen who were not addicted to the chase, and curiosity about them put a new light on her adventure. Papa had ridiculed the idea, she remembered, but logic told her that if her father seldom went to Town, had even an aversion to it, then perhaps those gentlemen who spent most of their time there were quite different. Sophie sat up in bed alert.

Sir Tony had winked at her. The strange thing was that she had not disliked it. He was not handsome, at least not in the florid, masculine way that her father had been as a young man, or the Prince Regent. But she did like the way he smiled at one, so openly, without reserve, and she had noticed, rather vaguely at first and more consciously later, that she liked the way he moved. He was tall and slender—but not lanky; at ease—but perfectly alert; relaxed—yet efficient. He had rather ordinary light brown hair and blue eyes, but he was pleasant to look at. It must be his constant expression of goodwill which she found so attractive. Surely no one with that smile could intend to do her ill with an improper wink.

Sophie went downstairs for breakfast hoping to see him again, but learned along with her parents that Sir Tony Farnham had left quite early that morning.

The rest of the day was busy enough to keep her keenly tuned to her surroundings, for the impact of London town upon the senses of one raised in the country was something she had not anticipated. Every turned corner offered glimpses of things of which she had never been aware, and even her father grew animated in pointing out objects of interest to her, from the Town mansions of the great aristocrats to the gallows at Tyburn. If it were not for an occasional recollection of their mission there, Sophie would have declared herself well pleased with the city.

They arrived in Berkeley Square and found themselves quite content with the house Sir John had taken for the season. The public rooms were spacious enough to permit small but adequate gatherings when they should be ready to entertain company. They spent the rest of the day unpacking, but during the afternoon, Lady Corby managed to dash off a note to Sir John's widowed sister, Mrs. Sarah Brewster, to let her know that they had arrived and were settling in. Mrs. Brewster had married a wealthy gentleman from Kent, who had left her a house in Town, his property in Kent and a small fortune to go with it. She, like her brother, was an avid enthusiast of the chase, but because of a severe fall incurred in her middle years, she had been forbidden to ride again. Since that time, she had seldom visited her brother in Leicestershire, preferring the amusements of London to sitting about the countryside watching others have all the fun.

But she was quite happy to receive her brother's family in Town and had written enthusiastically when she had heard of their plans to come. Soon after noon on the day following their arrival, she appeared, bursting in upon them like a whipper-in going after some wayward hounds.

"Hallo Clarissa!" she boomed, taking her sister-in-law in a crushing embrace. "You are looking much too pale, gel! Looks like you're off your feed." She subjected Lady Corby to a careful scrutiny. "Not breeding again, I hope? No? That's good. Where's that girl Sophie?" she asked, turning abruptly. "Let me see you! Just as I remembered you. You look fine, gel! In prime form! You will take well." She hugged Sophie mercilessly and patted her briskly on the back, while giving her a final bit of heartfelt advice. "Just don't rush your fences."

Though the sentiments were not what Sophie could wish, she had to smile. It was impossible not to like this bold, unconventional woman, even if she did not share one's tastes.

Lady Corby, however, was slightly overcome. Between visits she tended to forget the full effect of Mrs. Brewster's personality, and she might be forgiven for imagining that the experience of Town life might have had some moderating influence. Still, she, too, had an affection for her sister-in-law, despite their differences.

"Sadie," she said rather breathlessly, "you are looking well. I'm so glad you were at home to get our message."

"I wasn't," stated Aunt Sadie matter-of-factly. "Just got word this morning. But I loaded up and drove to Town immediately. Made it in record time, too, in this weather. I shall have it reported to the Four-in-Hand Club, even though they will not count it officially. It will give them something to aim at.'' She spoke without rancour.

"Oh, dear,'' said Lady Corby faintly. "I fear we have inconvenienced you dreadfully.''

Aunt Sadie was astonished. "Of course not, gel! Did I say so? I always welcome a challenge. You know that. But enough of this. Where is my bow-legged whelp of a brother?''

By this time the sound of her booming voice had brought Sir John downstairs, and as she spoke he had come up behind her. Taking his cue, he put a rough arm around her rather thick waist and gave her a suffocating hug.

"Who's this calling me bow-legged? Sadie, you have not changed a whit. Still game enough for anything, I'll warrant.''

A rosy hue spread over Sadie's rather rugged countenance. She gave Sir John a hardy slap on the chest, which nearly knocked him into the passageway. "Of course, I am, you impudent dog! There is more to life than fox-hunting, you know, though I miss it, of course. And as long as that cur of a doctor don't tell me otherwise, I aim to enjoy it.''

Lady Corby, fearful that an exchange of brotherly blows might lead to some breakage in the hired furniture, hastily suggested that they sit and chat. Surprisingly, they seemed to have no objection, so she breathed a sigh of relief. Then no more than a few moments passed before brother and sister were deep in discussion of the losses to Sir John's stable that year.

Sophie listened with only half an ear, letting her mind roam as she usually did during such discussions. Her thoughts over the past day and a half had tended to dwell on their host at the Black Swan. Her curiosity about him had only increased, and she wondered if she should see him again. But her mental wanderings were interrupted suddenly by the sound of a knock at the door, and presently the butler entered to announce a visitor. It was Sir Tony.

He strolled into the sitting room with that attractive ease Sophie had noted in him, tipping his beaver off and into his hand with one swift, graceful movement of head and wrist. Then resting with one hand on an elegant cane, he paused and scanned the room briefly before giving them all an engaging smile. Sophie's eyes widened, and she smiled shyly as Lady Corby rose to her feet to greet him.

"Sir Tony," she said in her gentle, welcoming way. "How kind of you to call on us so soon. However did you find us?"

He answered her readily, "I took the liberty of making a few inquiries about the square, Lady Corby. It was not really difficult. I hope I do not come before you are ready for visitors."

"No, no," she said. "Please do come in."

Sir John by now had risen to his feet with less than his wife's enthusiasm. "Farnham," he said, nodding briskly. "Let me make you known to my sister, Mrs. Brewster."

He started to extend his hand to Aunt Sadie, but she spoke quickly, "There is no need, John. I already know Sir Tony, though I did not know that you had made his acquaintance. What brings you here, you sly rascal?"

Lady Corby was rather startled by this familiar form of address, but Tony just grinned. "Why, I had hoped to find you here, Miss Sadie. I was fortunate enough to meet your brother and his family on the road, and I fancied I detected a resemblance."

Sadie scoffed, and Lady Corby could only be glad that her sister-in-law was not near enough to give Sir Tony one of her cuffs on the chest. "That is just like your impudence! More like you came hoping to see my niece. You may wipe that silly grin off your face. You are not a villain in the hen house, you know."

But Tony only grinned wider and turned to speak to Sophie, who was beginning to feel rather left out of his greeting. "I will confess," he said. "I am delighted to see Miss Corby in such fine health. Good day to you, Miss Corby."

Sophie was not used to gallantry, but she managed to smile without lowering her eyes. A dimple appeared briefly on one cheek, and Tony was gratified to find that she was interested enough by his coming to appear more alert than at their first meeting. He noticed, too, that the brighter light of day did nothing to diminish the tempting lure of Sophie's dimples.

Lady Corby invited Tony to sit down, and he placed himself diplomatically near the elder ladies. Before long, Sir John had resumed his lament over the losses to his stable.

"I lost Dolly this year, Sadie," he said. "I had meant to write you, but couldn't bring myself to put it to paper. Knew you would be upset."

"What happened?" his sister asked with evident dismay.

Sir John shook his head sadly. "Lost her flat out beneath me. It was a long run, near on two and three-quarter hours. Just too much for her finally, and near the beginning of the season—before she was in top form. If I had known we would have such a fine run that day, I would have taken one of the younger nags, but there was no way of knowing, of course," he said sadly. "The scent stayed strong throughout, even though we crossed two fallow fields in the course of the run. I feared she was flagging near the end, but of course, I could not abandon the chase. She took her last ditch flying. A sad business. I changed quickly to another mount to finish the run, of course, and sent my man to fetch her as soon as I reached him. He tried everything he could to save her, but she never made it back to the stable."

"Tragic business!" said Sadie, a hint of hoarseness in her voice. "I remember riding her myself, many times. When you first acquired her. Remember that great run I had on her in '06? The one where Percival Blakehollow broke his leg?''

Sir John perked up instantly. He smiled ruminatively. "Aye," he said. "That would have been the fifteenth November. I remember because I had the lead the following day and had to recount the whole to Percy who was laid up in bed. Dolly was a game one, wasn't she. Hated to lose her. Miracle she lasted that long, though, when you come to think of it. She had her share of great runs.''

Sophie's mind had wandered off again. She was disappointed that Sir Tony had placed himself so far from her chair and now feared that the conversation would never venture from the chase. He might not choose to call again, if he found them incapable of general discussion. She yawned openly, forgetting to cover her mouth, and her mother glanced at her with gentle reproach. But Sophie came to attention when she heard Tony speak. His expression throughout Sir John's tale had been once again polite and attentive.

"Did you hunt then, Miss Sadie?" he asked with true admiration.

"Of course, boy," answered Sadie, but she sighed. "T'was a bad fall that finished me.''

Sir John spoke proudly, "Sadie was a game girl, let me tell you. There never was a fence to stop her. My father said she was the best of us all, and all the Corbys hunt."

"Do you hunt, Lady Corby?" asked Tony, turning to face his hostess.

Lady Corby appeared rather ashamed and said weakly, "No, Sir Tony. I am afraid not. But with all the children to look after..."

"Of course," he hastened to reassure her. "I had not realized there were so many."

"Eight," said Sir John proudly, "and all the boys fine riders. Emma, too. All of them good Corbys, except Sophie here, who prefers to waste her time writing nonsense when she could be outdoors with the best of them." He looked at his daughter reproachfully.

"Enough of that, Sir John!" exclaimed Sadie. "As I remember, Sophie is a fine rider, and if she does not choose to break her neck with the rest of you, well—" and here, though she obviously could not comprehend it, she spoke justly "—then that is her affair. What is this about writing?" she asked Sophie.

Her niece squirmed uncomfortably under their stares. "It is nothing," she said dismissively. "I have just been attempting a bit of poetry."

"Poetry!" scoffed Sir John. But Tony came to her rescue quickly.

"That is admirable, Miss Corby," he said. "I am known to dabble in it myself, though my friends speak rather harshly of the result. They are so critical, in fact, that I may soon find myself reduced to the level of poet abstentious. I have decided to confine myself to birthday odes from now on."

"And dashed impudent ones, I'll warrant," said Sadie with a laugh. "Hardly fit for royalty! I would be surprised to see a serious sonnet come out of that head of yours."

Sir John did not appear to like the turn of the conversation. "Well, you fellows in Town get up to a deal of foolish nonsense, I know. But it beats me how Sophie can waste her time on poetry. It ought not to be in her blood. Clarissa comes from a long line of good hunting stock, and the children have all bred true but Sophie here." He sighed.

Sounds like a litter of puppies, thought Sophie. She had hoped that Sir Tony's comment would stop her father from expressing himself on her shortcomings in front of their guest, but, at least, now he seemed recalled to his manners enough to let the subject drop. While he reminisced further about his own father's prowess in the field, her mind wandered again, and she gazed out the window. The city outside was alive with activity, and she chafed against the social restraints which kept a maiden lady indoors. In the country, at least, she would have been free to go on a solitary walk, as was her habit. But here, despite the lure of strange delights in all she spied, she had to wait for a parent's escort. Sophie had to envy her Aunt Sadie her widow's freedom to drive herself about Town at will.

"I should like to learn to drive a phaeton about London," she said aloud suddenly to no one in particular. The others suspended their conversation, and her mother released a gentle, "Oh, dear."

"I'll teach you!" volunteered Aunt Sadie, in tones of hearty approval. "Be delighted to! I knew you had pluck, gel. Don't worry, Clarissa," she said as Lady Corby started to protest. "I'll not let any harm come to the gel. You know that."

"Speaking of riding out," said Tony, taking advantage of the opportunity. "I had rather hoped that Miss Corby would take a turn in the park with me today." Her sudden interjection had delighted him, coming as it did out of the blue, and he wondered what train of thought had brought her to that curious pronouncement. "That is, of course, if you have no objection," he added, speaking to Lady Corby.

Sophie looked up with budding delight, but her mother seemed to have grave doubts. She turned to Sir John for guidance.

"I do not know, Sir Tony. Wouldn't it seem rather particular? Sir John?"

But before Sophie's father could refuse the plan, Aunt Sadie came once again to the rescue. "Nonsense! It's a capital idea! And it will not seem in the least particular, I assure you, Clarissa. Everyone permits it nowadays. You would not have her set down as a country miss. Besides, she cannot be ravished in an open phaeton, after all—at least not in the park. Pay attention to his ribbons, Sophie. He can show you a thing or two. Capital whip!"

Lady Corby hastily gave her consent, hoping to cut off any more shocking statements from her sister-in-law, and Sophie ran upstairs to fetch her bonnet and pelisse and to submit to a quick hairbrushing while Tony responded modestly to Sadie's last remark.

"You flatter me, Miss Sadie."

"Nonsense!" she said, raising her eyebrows in admonition. "You could be admitted to the Four-Horse Club at a moment's notice if you wished. Everyone says so. Why don't you do it?"

Tony smiled mysteriously and shook his head as Sophie joined them once again. "Above my touch I'm afraid," he said, holding Sophie's pelisse for her. And he politely refused to be drawn back into the conversation, though Sadie continued to remonstrate with him. Taking up his beaver, he promised to have Sophie back in due time, and they made their way out of the room.

The door had scarcely closed behind them when Sir John let loose his indignation, "Frippery fellow, that! Poetry! I ask you, what does he mean by it?"

"Oh, don't let him fool you, John," said Sadie. "That boy can do anything. He just chooses to play the fool at times, though I don't know why. He's a spanking whip, and they tell me he's a competent pugilist, too. He just don't choose to brag about it, I suppose."

"But he said himself he does not hunt!" complained Sir John. "Perhaps he cannot afford it. I don't want him hanging out after Sophie if he does not have the blunt to support her.''

"It's not that," said Sadie, shaking her head in perplexity. "He is said to have a good £10,000 a year or more.''

"He could manage on that, though I suppose it might be a bit tight. There's many a better does it on less," he added stubbornly.

"His father was quite a sporting gentleman," remembered Sadie. "Addicted to the turf, as I remember. Nearly ruined his estate. Perhaps Tony don't care to do the same.''

But Sir John would not allow it. "That's ridiculous! He needn't support his own stables, and you know it. He could always hire a hack. That's coming it a bit strong, Sadie. I don't see why you need defend the fellow. He's little better than a coxcomb! Did you see that cane?''

Sadie knew her defense sounded weak to her sporting-enthusiast brother, but she stood her ground. "Perhaps there is no understanding it, John," she sighed impatiently. "But you are wrong about Tony. Whatever his faults, I cannot help but like the man.''

CHAPTER THREE

THE OBJECT OF THEIR DISCUSSION was at this moment turning his team of high spirited horses in the direction of Hyde Park with a skillful flick of his whip. He managed to keep up a spanking pace and still catch a glimpse of his companion out the corner of one eye. Sophie was regarding the horses in front of her with fixed attention. Though it might not be thought particular in London for a single lady to ride out with a gentleman alone, she was thinking that it seemed very particular to her. She had never been alone with a strange gentleman before, if you could call sitting atop a high perch phaeton in the middle of a busy London street "being alone."

Tony's lips twitched understandingly as he watched her in silence, noting the softness of lowered lashes against her cheeks. But presently he ventured a question. "Are you paying careful attention to the ribbons, as your aunt suggested, Miss Corby? I shall be glad to give you instruction as we go along."

Sophie blushed delightfully, but was glad for the excuse to talk. "Yes," she said with little honesty. "I do not see how you manage to keep them so steady."

"There is no trick to it," said Tony. "You must simply keep the reins to your leaders separate from those to your wheelers so that you may direct them separately—just so." He showed her which fingers to lace the reins through so as to hold them properly. Of course, this obliged Sophie to look up at him and to observe his actions minutely. She began to enjoy herself.

After watching him negotiate a narrow space between a milkcart and a bookseller's stall, she remembered his final conversation with her Aunt Sadie and a suspicion that had then crossed her mind. So she asked, "Don't you wish to be a member of the Four-Horse Club, Sir Tony?" Her own brothers had such strong aspirations to that honour that she was again mystified.

Tony looked more apologetic than ever as he answered, but she thought she detected a twinkle in his eyes. "I see you have discovered my secret, Miss Corby. But if you will promise not to reveal it to any of the club's members, I shall be happy to explain."

She nodded in agreement.

"You will think me a worthless fellow, I know," he went on, "but the truth is that I do not want to be obliged to parade to Salt Hill on certain days of the month dressed in a curious habit. I should find the requirement rather tedious.''

Sophie dimpled by way of reply, but did not tell him that he had delighted her again. Instead, folding her hands in her lap, she looked about her with a sigh of satisfaction, as Tony grinned appreciatively.

Presently she asked, "Where are you taking me?''

"To Rotten Row," was the reply.

She looked at him in astonishment. "I thought you said you were taking me to the park!''

Tony, who had taken a moment to understand her surprise, chuckled pleasantly. "I *am* taking you to the park, Miss Corby. I suppose the name does sound rather suspicious if one is not used to hearing it, but I assure you that Rotten Row is a very respectable lane along Hyde Park. At this time of day there will be any number of the most fashionable people there on horse or in carriage—and some less so, I might add. I thought it might amuse you on your first day to see one of the fashionable strolls. You might even glimpse the Prince Regent.''

"Oh," said Sophie with visible relief. "I thought..." She did not finish.

"That your Aunt Sadie might have been wrong, perhaps?'' said Tony, before adding cryptically, "I shall await your permission for that.''

By the time Sophie had digested this comment and thought to blush, they had arrived at the park and Tony had changed the subject. He began to point out persons of interest to her as he slowed the pace of his horses. She had to admire the ease with which he kept them under control while conversing, not seeming to have them much in mind.

"Who are those young men over there?" Sophie asked. "The ones who all seem to be yawning. Could they be bored with Town life already?"

Tony cocked an eye at them. "Those are what we call 'peep-o-day boys,'" he said. "They are out-and-out larkers. They spend their nights on the prowl for adventure, not going to bed until morning, so that this time of day they are just waking—or trying to, by the looks of them."

"What do they find to do all night?" asked Sophie. The notion was intriguing.

"Oh, there are any number of strange, wild things to do in the streets at night," he answered. "What was it the Scotch poet said? 'Here are we met three merry boys,/ three merry boys I trow are we. /And mony a night we've merry been,/ and mony mae we hope to be.'" Sophie smiled as he went on.

"There is much to be said for it really, although I'm afraid that the greater number of those fellows spend the night getting progressively drunker, until there's not much that they would recall. But after the theatre or the opera or a ball, there are curious things to be seen in the less fashionable quarters of the city. There are the coffee houses or sluiceries—for gin, you know—where one meets up with all walks of life. You might see a beggar, whom you saw hobbling on crutches near Temple Bar that morning, dance a jig with the proprietress at night. There are places in St. Giles where all manner of such revelations take place.

"But I suspect that those boys simply drink their fill of gin, some losing their purses to the pickpockets which are found in every public place, until they stagger out into the street and start a row. There, see that fellow just there? I suspect he is one of them." He jerked his head over toward a group of people standing on the side of the lane.

"Where?" asked Sophie. Then spying the man he had indicated she said, "That stiff gentleman standing on the corner? Is he a peep-o-day boy, too? He doesn't look sleepy, and he seems too proper for what you were relating."

Tony laughed, but in the kind way he had. "No, not a peep-o-day boy. A pickpocket. And the reason he appears so stiff is because he is gammoning the draper."

"What does that mean?" asked Sophie suspiciously. She was not at all sure that he was not teasing her.

"That is just a cant expression. It means that he is concealing the fact that he has no shirt. See the way his coat is buttoned up so tightly, straight up to his neckcloth? That is so you will not notice the absence of shirt and waistcoat beneath."

Sophie did not know whether to be impressed or suspicious. She still thought he might be teasing her. Looking over at the object of their discussion once again, she asked, "How do you know that? He appears quite normal to me."

Tony's smile expressed such satisfaction with her that she had to believe him. "That is what he hopes you will think. Don't you see? He would not be much good at his trade if his tricks were too obvious. He has to be able to fool the green ones, at least." Sophie supposed he was including her in this category, but his next words removed all offense.

"The reason I can detect him is because I've lost enough to persons of his brotherhood to make me more knowing. And I've met up with them again in such places where their masks were down."

As he said this, a new thought occurred to Sophie. "Are *you* a peep-o-day boy, Sir Tony?" she asked glancing up at him shyly.

She thought she heard him smother a laugh, but he answered her seriously enough. "No, Miss Corby, I am not."

There was more Sophie would have asked him, but she was afraid he would laugh at her ignorance, so she looked about the park again in what she thought a worldly-wise fashion. As she did so, she noted that a middle-aged woman with three elegant young females in a handsome equipage was waving in their direction. Sophie turned quickly to Tony and said, "Pardon me, but that lady in the handsome carriage seems to know you. She is trying to capture your attention.''

Tony leaned forward in his seat to see whom she was speaking of, but immediately returned to his position. "She must be mistaken,'' he said with a suspicious twist to his lips. "I do not recall having met her.''

"Are you certain?'' Sophie persisted, looking once again at the ladies and smiling uncertainly. "She has not stopped waving. She has three young ladies with her. I suppose they are her daughters. Perhaps if we drove closer you might recognize her.''

Tony cleared his throat and turned the phaeton in the opposite direction. "I do not think that would be wise, Miss Corby. Your father would surely object.''

"But why?'' asked Sophie.

The horses had settled into a comfortable trot again, so Tony could face her more easily. There was an unmistakable grin on his face. "Let us just say that although I have not met them, I recognize them sufficiently to know that they would not be proper acquaintances for you—though you will come into contact with some who are no better. Those are not the lady's daughters riding with her. They are more in the nature of employees.''

"But they are dressed quite as elegantly as she,'' protested Sophie stubbornly.

Her persistence seemed to delight him, and he finally let loose with laughter. "Miss Corby,'' he asked her, "has no one told you that you would be wiser not to pursue a topic when you've been offered polite evasions? It would truly not be proper of me to elucidate the matter fully, though if you insist, I shall. But you must not report me to your parents if I do, for I gave you ample and fair warning.''

Sophie sat for a minute and reflected. Certainly her mother would wish for her to desist, but a glance at Tony's face decided her. There was something rather alluring in the way he looked at her, as though he dared her to question him. She was reminded of that first night's wink and her flight up the stairs.

Folding her hands in her lap demurely, she tried to strike a reasoning attitude. ''It seems to me, Sir Tony,'' she said, ''that you have taken it upon yourself to caution me and instruct me in the ways of the city. If there is something I ought to know to protect myself against improper associations, I can only take it as a kindness in you to inform me.'' She looked at him as a schoolmistress might when expecting a pupil to recite a lesson.

She must have caught him unprepared, however, for he was sufficiently distracted to allow the horses to stray near an on-coming vehicle and a few moments passed before he brought them back into line. By that time, he had managed to conceal his amusement and could answer her in approximately the same tone of scientific inquiry that she had employed.

''Very well. The person who was beckoning to us from the carriage yonder is what is commonly called a procuress.'' Tony kept his gaze on his horses as he spoke. "The young women with her are her ware. You will hear them referred to as Cyprians in fashionable society. Their 'mother,' she may be called, dresses them elegantly to lure their customers and in exchange receives the greater part of their earnings. Now, if I have not made things sufficiently clear at this point, Miss Corby, I will be unequal to the task of making it clearer. I would suggest that you ask your Aunt Sadie to explain the term 'Cyprian' to you at a future date.'' Then pausing significantly, he added, "*Not* telling her, of course, who put you up to it.'' He smiled at her now with a questioning tilt to his head.

Somewhere during his discourse, Sophie had come to comprehend what he was saying, though she had to question whether she had listened properly. It was certainly shocking if she had! But she did not intend to make Sir Tony regret his honesty by appearing to be unsettled. Swallowing before answering, she merely said, "Thank you. That will not be necessary.''

She thought she detected another twitch of his lips before he turned to face the horses. She was uncomfortably silent for a while, but presently a thought popped into her head which refused to be silenced.

"It was still uncommonly odd the way they appeared to know *you*, Sir Tony.''

Her companion coughed so suddenly and so violently that his horses took great exception and began to plunge and rear. It took Tony several minutes to calm them sufficiently and when he did, it was with no reference at all to her comment.

"Pardon me, Miss Corby. A mere catch in the throat." He resumed speaking about the people they were passing, and Sophie allowed him to change the subject, though she dimpled wickedly.

As they had been out for some time now, Tony suggested returning to her parents' house, and although Sophie had no wish to end the excursion, she had to agree. Perhaps she had received enough information to digest for one day, but her curiosity on one point begged an answer.

"Sir Tony," she began in a perplexed tone as he turned the horses back toward Town, "If you are not a peep-o-day boy and you do not hunt, what *do* you do?"

Tony seemed taken aback. He appeared to be at a loss for words, but he chuckled and, after considering, responded, "Why, everything else, I suppose."

"And what, pray, is everything else?" demanded Sophie.

He laughed again. "Oh, just anything you can imagine. I see no reason to confine myself to one pursuit or another. There is no end to the things that interest me. I've told you that I write poetry, though I'm no good at it. But I do attend salons where people of talent come together to enlighten one another. I shall take you to one one day. And even though I do not hunt, I still admire a good horse and enjoy going to

Tattersall's occasionally. I go to the theatre, the opera, and—yes, even the coffee and gin houses on occasion. And the boxing matches and so on. I guess you
could say that I am an observer rather than a player,
such as your father. I had rather hear about what he
does than spend my entire life devoted to it. It amuses
me to listen to his stories.''

Sophie was not certain how to take his last comment. He seemed so much more a part of the fashionable world than anyone else she knew, and
remembering her father's opinions about the artifi-
ciality of the social elite, she began to worry.

''Does that mean that you dine out on anecdotes
about my father and my aunt and people like that?''

Tony glanced at her, and the smile left his face.
Then, he carefully pulled his horses over to the side of
the street and brought them to rest. Turning to face her,
he spoke very gently.

''You must not think that I amuse myself at the expense of people like your father, Miss Corby. I would
never be so unkind as to make him the object of my
humour. In fact, I admire him in a way. It takes courage to run the risk of breaking your neck every day—
certainly more than I have.'' He smiled at her again,
and Sophie was ashamed for having said what she did.
Hadn't she already observed that there was no mean-
ness in him? She flushed uncomfortably and lowered
her eyes as he continued.

"Now, having said that, and being a truthful fellow, I will add—just between you and me—that I find Sir John and your Aunt Sadie terribly amusing."

Sophie looked up again quickly and seeing the fun in his eyes, she dimpled. Then she thought of her father and Aunt Sadie as if seeing them for the first time with all their odd expressions and attitudes, and she began to giggle. "I suppose they are," she said. "It is just that when one has grown up surrounded by only sporting enthusiasts, it is hard to see the humour in them. But now that I know not everyone is like that, I can see how funny they must seem to you."

"I understand," said Tony. "My father was one of them. But my mother is quite a different story. I will take you to meet her one day. You will like her." He took up the reins again and headed the horses toward Berkeley Square. Sophie thanked him for his offer, feeling the full compliment of the gesture. She wondered if he would really take her there and why he should want to.

"Since we are being so forthright with our curiosity today, Miss Corby," he said presently, "perhaps you could answer a question for me."

"Certainly."

"Why is it that you look so uncomfortable when anyone talks about your coming out? Do you not like the prospect?"

Sophie gave a big sigh. "Oh, that. Well, I suppose it may be fun to go to assemblies and such things and to meet new people, like you. But my father has made it quite clear that this will be my only chance to marry, you see. So I must be married by the end of the season or he shall marry me off to someone of his own choosing. He does not wish to waste another season away from his hunting.''

"And you do not wish to be married? Is that it?''

"I didn't think so,'' began Sophie, "at least not before I met..." She broke off suddenly, realizing that what she had been about to say might sound terribly odd, though she had only meant that meeting Sir Tony had taught her that there were other kinds of gentlemen than the ones she was used to. She fancied he looked at her strangely, so she went on. "That is, I do not want to marry just for the sake of being off Papa's hands. I do not want to go to live with someone with whom I have nothing in common."

Tony smiled understandingly. She found it hard to resist smiling back. "No," he said, "you must certainly not do that." But seeing that a certain bleakness was returning to her face, he assured her, "Please do not worry. You will meet many interesting people here, and I shall hope that one of them will strike your fancy."

"But what if that does not happen?" Sophie asked.

They had turned on to the square by now, and Tony pulled the horses over to the curb. "Then someone," he said mysteriously, "will be seriously disappointed."

CHAPTER FOUR

THE NEXT FEW DAYS were busy ones. Sophie and her mother went all over Town calling on old acquaintances and shopping for trimmings to gowns, reticules and pelisses. They were careful to stay within the budget Sir John had given them, for he would not likely be pleased if Sophie's London season cost him more than he had planned. While they were out on their errands, Sir John himself spent his time at Boodle's or looking in on the sales at Tattersall's. He was finding that there was much pleasure to be had in meeting up with other fox-hunting devotees who had been dragged to Town by their wives, and there was something to be said for being able to drop in on the sales when a prime horse was likely to be sold.

After one morning spent in such a fashion, Sir John came home to find his wife and daughter returned with their purchases from the day's shopping. He instantly asked to inspect the bills and was outraged at the sum.

"French gloves," he exclaimed, "lace, ribbons— what is all this, Clarissa? And look at this—yards and yards of poplin at 4s, 5d from Layton & Shear's! And brocade! I thought we had Sophie's clothes made before we left home so they wouldn't cost so much, and now you seem to be starting all over again!'' Sir John's face was quite red.

Lady Corby had not expected his objection, and she was taken aback, but she tried to answer calmly. ''Her gowns *were* made at home, Sir John. But we could not find the trimmings back in the village. These will be added to Sophie's dresses to make them more attractive. And I'm afraid the poplin is for me. If I am going to accompany Sophie to her engagements, I must have something to wear that will not embarrass her.''

''But what about these gloves and the brocade?'' he insisted.

''Now, dear,'' pleaded Lady Corby, ''you must remember that you gave us permission to have a ball gown made here in London so we could see just what the fashions are. And it was good planning for us to wait, for we have learned that gowns are not so much off the shoulder as they were, and we would not have Sophie appear different. And,'' she added, ''a good pair of gloves is a must, and they are not to be had at this price at home.''

Sir John was shaking his head in defeat. It was clear that he thought he had been betrayed. ''I don't know, Clarissa. I just don't know. It all seems so frivolous. I daresay that Sophie will be engaged before the month is out, and we shall find that all of this expense could have been avoided. It comes at a devilish bad time, too.''

The worry in his voice alarmed Lady Corby, and Sophie, too, felt a pang of conscience that she might be overstretching the family income.

"What is it, Sir John?" her mother asked anxiously. "What is wrong? Why is this a particularly bad time?"

Sir John regarded them both with an air of reproach. "Because I have just purchased a new nag," he said impressively. "Had to pay top price for him, too. The bidding at Tattersall's was fierce, but I had it on good authority that he was a prize not to be missed. Lord Kemple assured me that he had put him over many a fence six feet and higher with never a miss. Only had to sell him because it's either that or face the bailiff. He's all to pieces.'' Sir John shook his head in commiseration.

Lady Corby glanced at Sophie, and Sophie saw a look in her mother's eyes that she had never seen before. It was as though something was suddenly clear. Lady Corby turned once again to her husband.

"It astonishes me, Sir John," she said with unaccustomed firmness, "that you would complain about poplin at 4s, 5d when you have just bought another horse for £750!"

"But it was £850!" he exclaimed in a tone of perfect reason.

"Eight hundred fifty pounds, then," repeated Lady Corby. "I thought you said you were not going to make any additions to your stables this year, since you would not be at home to use them until next November."

Her reasoning did not seem to carry with Sophie's father. "That is beside the point, Clarissa. What I am saying is that these purchases of bows and ribbons and—and furbelows have got to be kept within bounds. I will not have this family paying on tick. It shall be bills paid with us or we simply cannot have things. I have no wish to end up like Kemple, now. Do you?"

Lady Corby sighed in exasperation, "Certainly not, Sir John. But it would surprise me if Lady Kemple's ribbon merchant had very much to do with it."

Sir John looked at her suspiciously, but declined to discuss the point. "That is neither here nor there, Clarissa. The point is that all these purchases add up. I will not have my estate frittered away with extravagances; it happens all too often these days, and if it happens to us, well, I do not think you would like to blame yourself." His eyes widened suddenly with a hopeful thought. "I suppose you could return some of these things?"

Lady Corby drew herself up with offended dignity. "No, Sir John, I could not. But perhaps you could take your new hunter back to Tattersall's."

Her husband's chest swelled alarmingly as he drew in his breath. His expression of outrage was comical. "Madam, I am shocked that you could suggest such a thing! That horse may well prove to be the finest in my stud. And how you could expect me to get along with less than twelve hunters now that Dolly is gone, I cannot imagine. Do you think I would pay such a price for it if I were not reasonably assured of getting a good few seasons out of it?'' Sir John's frustration with the poor understanding of his wife and daughter was pitiable.

He picked up his hat and pulled it down firmly on his head. ''I am going to my club,'' he said loudly, ''and I do not expect to be back before dinner. Perhaps *there* I will find someone who can talk sense.'' He marched to the door and after giving them one more offended look over his shoulder, stormed out.

Sophie had watched this whole scene with a mixture of emotions: surprise that her mother had taken a firm stand against her father's position, dismay, since the quarrel had been about purchases for herself, and frustration over the illogic of the argument. But as her father walked angrily out the door, she remembered Tony's smile when he confided to her that he found her father rather amusing. And immediately, the absurdity of her father's position struck her. The door had barely closed when she began to giggle.

Lady Corby looked at her in surprise. She had been feeling very ill-used. ''Sophia!'' she exclaimed.

Sophie stopped giggling immediately, but with difficulty. ''I'm sorry, Mama. It was just that Papa...'' She paused, uncertain how to explain. ''He was so—

absurd!'' Her mouth quivered with suppressed laughter.

Lady Corby regarded her with amazement. ''Sophie,'' she began, ''I am shocked to hear you refer to your father in such . . .'' but she did not finish. The mirth in her daughter's eyes seemed to affect her strangely. Her posture, which had been stiffly erect throughout the exchange with Sir John, relaxed, her expression softened and she smiled reluctantly. ''I suppose he is rather ridiculous whenever anything threatens his hunting. I had not thought of it that way,'' she admitted. ''But he has never overreached his income to pay for it,'' she reminded Sophie justly. ''We have always been able to count on him for whatever we need and know that the bailiffs will not be at the door. This is the first time I have been resentful of his extravagances in the field. But,'' she added firmly, ''I will not let him be so extravagant that we cannot present you in the proper style.''

Some of Sophie's earlier emotions returned. She sobered instantly. ''I am sorry, Mama, if our coming to London will be the cause of any discord between you.''

Lady Corby patted her hand lovingly, then returned to unpacking their parcels in better cheer. ''Never think of it, my dear. Your father will likely find a sympathetic companion at his club, and by the time they have discussed the merits and defects of his recent purchase thoroughly, he will be restored to good humour.''

Sophie's anxious frown cleared immediately. She giggled again. "Let's hope he doesn't find that he has bought a crammer, or we might get blamed for that, too." Her mother declined to answer, but lifted her eyebrows expressively.

Fortunately, however, Sir John returned to his home an hour before dinnertime restored to good humour as predicted. He appeared to have forgotten the altercation completely.

Greeting his wife and daughter in the parlour where he found them, he sat down with an air of satisfaction. "Clarissa, my dear," he announced. "I have invited a gentleman to dinner. Sophie, you will need to put on one of your prettiest gowns. This fellow merits all the attention you can give him."

Lady Corby looked up from her sewing with interest. "What is this, Sir John? A new acquaintance or someone you already know?"

"Just met him today, my love," answered her husband. "But took to him right away. He's just the kind of fellow I'd hoped we'd find for Sophie, though I'd not much hope of it here in London. He's what you would call a complete hand! A Corinthian! Awake on every suit. Sophie could not do better."

Sophie's spirits sank. She doubted that she and her father would be struck equally by a gentleman's qualities, so she sought her mother's aid with a pleading look.

Lady Corby understood the message. "Let's not be hasty, Sir John," said she gently. "We will be delighted to meet him, of course, but since you have just met the gentleman, perhaps we should know more about him before we make any judgement."

Sir John's good humour was not diminished by this lack of confidence. "Oh, we will take our time, naturally. But wait until Sophie sees the fellow. Then she will thank her old father." He lay back in his chair with a smug expression.

Sophie smiled at him weakly.

An hour later she was making her curtsey before a tall, athletically built young man, and she had to admit that he looked much more promising than she could possibly have believed. He was handsome and polished, well-dressed and well-mannered. As he was introduced, he bent over her hand with an accomplished bow, but he was, she fancied, more impressed with his own performance than with any appearance of hers.

"My daughter Sophia, Mr. Rollo," her father was saying. "A fine girl, if I may say so, and out in society just recently."

Mr. Rollo bowed again in her direction with just the right touch of admiration in his expression. "Then I count myself fortunate that I should be in Town this season. Indeed, the whole city of London should count itself fortunate," he added with a little smile at this pleasantry.

Sophie blushed uncomfortably. She did not know how to respond to this extravagant form of flattery and was not certain that she liked it. But her mother and father both looked pleased, and there was nothing in Mr. Rollo's manner that could be considered offensive. She smiled prettily and said nothing.

She need not have feared that her father would embarrass her at the dinner table by extolling her qualities for Mr. Rollo as though she were on the auction block, for Sir John was much more impressed with their guest. He repeated what he had learned about Mr. Rollo that day as they sat over their joint of beef.

"A fine sportsman you must be, Rollo, to be a member of the Four-in-Hand Club." Their guest was gratified.

"It would be wrong in me to boast, Sir John, but I cannot deny the excellent driving ability of our members. Sir John Lade, of course, has such a reputation with his fine team of matched greys that I need not describe them for you, but the others do quite as well with perhaps not the same style. I feel fortunate to be among them," he finished modestly.

Sophie told herself she should be pleased by his modest answer to the question, but somehow she was not struck that way.

"Have you other interests, Mr. Rollo?" she ventured to ask.

He regarded her indulgently. "Yes, Miss Corby. I have many, and perhaps you ladies would rather converse on topics other than sport. I can assure you of having more cultivated interests," he said with a smirk. "For example, I am not a small collector of fine art works. My apartments are amply furnished with both beautiful paintings and noble pieces of craftsmanship. I fancy myself something of a connoisseur in that line. Perhaps you would accompany me one day to the Royal Academy. I would be delighted to show you the galleries and trust that my comments will not be entirely unwelcome instruction." He looked around the table for a response.

Lady Corby smiled agreeably. "That sounds delightful." She glanced at Sophie and finding nothing in her expression to discourage her, accepted the invitation on her daughter's behalf. A date was fixed, and Sophie was not displeased. As yet, she had seen little of London and an afternoon at the Royal Academy sounded rather grand. She looked on Mr. Rollo more favourably.

Their guest continued to impress them with his mastery of the city's amusements, the opera, the theatre, the assemblies, until dessert was served. Then Sir John, who had been listening patiently with the obvious air of promoting his daughter's acquaintance with Mr. Rollo, took charge of the conversation again.

"Rollo," he said, "I was not able to finish telling you, this afternoon, about the astuteness of our master of hounds, Mr. Bentham, of whom you have heard such reports. I believe that one anecdote will illustrate just what I mean when I say that he is without equal.''

Mr. Rollo turned to him with interest. Sir John continued. ''It was December seventeen of last year, I believe, when we were following the pack at a furious speed. The hounds had outdistanced us when they set off down the steep bank of a stream after the fox, and all of us who were still in the field had to go thirty yards out of the way to find a place to ford. The next fence was a rasper and put us farther behind, but the pack was in full pursuit, and we could hear them sounding. Their perfection showed in their hard running, heads up, tails down. It was fine to behold. (Bentham has never had a hound quit the chase!) Anyway, as I was saying, we heard the cry of the leader. And Bentham, who was keeping pace with me at the time, says, 'That will be Patch in the lead.' He spoke with full confidence. I assure you that we were so far behind the pack that I had to wonder how he could distinguish the cries, but as we caught up to them, Bentham's huntsman, as fine a man as ever held that position, confirmed it. He had thought it another hound, but Bentham proved to be right!'' And to emphasize the astounding nature of his story, Sir John brought his hand down on the table with a loud slap.

The slap caught Sophie, whose thoughts had drifted, unawares. Her head jerked so forcefully that she was certain their guest must have noticed it, but glancing in his direction, she realized that he had not. He was giving his full attention to her father, and his expression was so rapt with fascination that her heart sank within her. An inner voice cried, "Oh, no."

Sir John was still speaking about his master of hounds. "He breeds hard-to-line, of course. Won't allow bow-legged blood to enter in, even if it means sacrificing strong scenting ability to speed. He has to hang many a pup, but, of course, it's necessary."

"Of course," agreed Mr. Rollo without a blink.

"I give him free walking rights over all my own properties. He has not enough to exercise the hounds properly during cubbing season. He don't let them kill the foxes in cover mind you, for a seasoned fox is as necessary to the hunt as a seasoned hound, I always say."

"I could not agree with you more, Sir John," said Mr. Rollo. He sighed. "I must say I envy you your county of residence. I have hunted from Melton Mowbray, and it was the greatest pleasure of my life, but it takes means to maintain one's own stud so far away from one's home county."

"Have you not the income for it, my boy?" asked Sir John sympathetically.

"Alas, no," said Mr. Rollo. "Not yet. But do not think my prospects are without hope," he added, remembering the presence of the ladies. "I am fortunate to have a doting aunt who has the intention of making me her heir. She will be leaving me quite well off, and I have reason to hope she will not last out the year."

"That is splendid, my boy!" cried Sir John. "We will drink to the prospect of seeing you in Leicestershire before the year is out."

"That is very kind of you, Sir John," smirked Mr. Rollo. "Would that I had not even so short a time to wait. I would not be kicking up my heels in London were it so. I have given serious thoughts to borrowing against my expectations so that the wait might be foregone. I have made it known in the city that my future looks bright, and it has stood me in good stead with tradesmen."

Sir John sobered instantly. "I advise you strongly not to do so, Rollo. I would not post-obit the old girl under any circumstances. Life is not so short that you cannot afford to wait one more season, but if it should get back to your aunt that you have traded on the prospect of her death, who's to say that she might not get offended and change her bequest. Women can take queer offences." He shrugged philosophically.

Mr. Rollo looked disturbed. "I had not thought of that, Sir John. I am most sincerely in your debt for having warned me. And you are right, of course. One more year will not make such a difference that I should risk all. And besides," he added, "I am not so much in debt that I cannot hunt with reasonable frequency."

Sophie's little voice proved to have spoken wisely, for as long as the ladies remained at table, Sir John and Mr. Rollo talked about hunting. They discussed everything from the best ground cover for pheasants to the desirable qualities in brood mares. And engrossed as he was by these topics, Mr. Rollo must have forgotten the ladies' presence entirely, for he did not once turn in their direction until Lady Corby rose to leave the table. Then, without apology for ignoring them so long, he rose also and bowed.

"I hope you will join us in the parlour afterward, Mr. Rollo," said Lady Corby. "Perhaps we can entertain you with a game of whist. I'm afraid we did not bring our pianoforte to Town, or Sophia would gladly have played for you."

"I shall come with all eagerness, Lady Corby," their guest promised, "although Miss Corby's playing will be sadly missed. Perhaps she will do me the honour of playing once for me in Leicestershire." He smiled at Sophie condescendingly.

Sophie inclined her head, though she doubted privately if, when once in Leicestershire, Mr. Rollo would have much inclination for music. She and her mother then swept gracefully from the table and withdrew to the parlour.

Lady Corby seated herself by the fire, which had just been lighted by the parlourmaid, and took up her embroidery. She did not speak at first, but presently, looking over her work at Sophie, she smiled reminiscently and said, "I must admit to being pleasantly surprised with our guest this evening. He seems to be a well-cultivated young man," she said on a leading note.

"Ye—es," Sophie responded with uncertainty.

"He rather reminds me of your father as a young man," her mother confided. "He was so strong and handsome." She sighed and shrugged her shoulders.

Sophie could not help but be alarmed at the comparison. She reflected for a moment before asking hesitantly, "Mama, have you never wished that Papa were, perhaps less interested in sport and more inclined to spend time with you?"

Her mother's smile faded as she put down her needlework. "Sophie," she said gently, "I must caution you not to be too romantic in your notions of marriage. You will find that men are but human. Why, the first time I saw your father astride a horse, as dashing as he seemed—almost as handsome as the Prince Regent was then—I thought I had met someone of heroic proportions. But that was a fairy-tale dream." Then Lady Corby added kindly, "But I do not mean to sadden you. Once you have children you will have your hands and your heart so full that you will scarcely notice whether your husband is with you or not.

"We just must be certain that you are marrying someone who will live within his means. He may have his stables and his coverts so long as he provides for you and your children. That should be your primary concern, and your father and I will try to make certain of it."

Sophie listened with swelling dismay. It saddened her to think that having children should be the only pleasure in marriage. Her mother had just admitted as much in reference to her own. She pondered before asking, "But what if I marry a man who has no wish to set up his stable?"

Lady Corby had just begun to stitch a new piece, but her hand stopped when Sophie uttered this question. "Not wish to...?" she began, and then paused. She laughed uncertainly. "Why, I never have given thought to such a circumstance," said Lady Corby finally. "After all, your father and my father and my grandfather.... I don't suppose I have known of any such men. But I have nothing to say against it. Of course, your father might find it hard to reconcile to having a son-in-law who showed so little interest in hunting, but perhaps he would not mind so much if the gentleman had a splendid fortune. Not set up his stable..." she trailed off, lost in wonder.

Sophie did not interrupt her mother's stitching again for she had her own thoughts to absorb her. She took up a basket of mending and worked at it sporadically between daydreams. From time to time, the sound of laughter or a song would come from the dining room, but the gentlemen showed no signs of joining them in the parlour. Finally, when the clock struck eleven o'clock, Sophie and her mother distinctly heard the familiar scream, or view-halloo, which, for Sir John at least, was a sure indication that more than four bottles of port had been drunk. Laying down her work with a sigh, Lady Corby rose to her feet.

"Come along, my dear," she said with resignation. "I fear the gentlemen will not be joining us this evening."

CHAPTER FIVE

HAVING COME TO LONDON very rarely in the course of their marriage, the Corbys had few near acquaintances in Town. Lady Corby and Sophie had been to visit those that Lady Corby could call upon as friends of her girlhood, some of whom she had written intermittently over the years. But she found that twenty years had done much to soften the ties of old friendship and few of these ladies could be counted on to help her introduce her daughter into society. Consequently, it was with total dependence that she turned to her greatest hope of presenting Sophie in the proper style. Almack's.

It might be thought that a family so long buried in the country would not have the connections to aspire to admittance to such an exclusive assemblage. But Sir John was confident. This was one accomplishment for which Sophie and her mother had to rely on him completely. Sir John had made the best of all possible connections for them in the field in Leicestershire, both the fourth Lord Jersey and the present earl when he was Lord Villiers, whose wife was now the greatest hostess in London. Armed with this introduction, Lady Corby and Sophie had called upon the Countess and found her to be as gay, imperious and energetic as everyone described her. She agreed to give Sophie her approval, and the two ladies returned home hopeful of receiving applications for vouchers within a few days.

Lady Corby was more delighted at the prospect, however, than her daughter was. Although Sophie agreed that admission to Almack's would afford her the best possible introduction to society and to acceptable young men, there was still a part of her that wanted nothing to do with the social set. For, while she could be lively when her interest was aroused, Sophie was still a private person. She spent a great deal of time daydreaming and composing her poetry. Her difference from her brothers and sister, though based on taste rather than temperament, had been clear enough to isolate her from her boisterous surroundings. And a London crowd held as much potential discomfort for her as the crowd at the Corbys' own dinner table.

So it was at times with a feeling of being sent to the gallows that Sophie faced such a grand introduction to the world.

But she might have spared herself the anxiety, for the response was not what the Corbys had expected. They were seated in the parlour, a few days after having made their call upon Lady Jersey, when a message was sent round from the Countess herself. Sir John was reading his paper when the note was brought in by the footman, but he put it aside and prepared to listen smugly while Lady Corby read it.

"Open it up, Clarissa," he said grandly, "and we'll see what her ladyship has to say to her papa-in-law's old friend."

Lady Corby opened the note with an expectant smile on her face, but it quickly vanished. "Oh, dear," she said in dismay.

"What is it?" Sir John asked.

Lady Corby looked up from the letter. "It says that she regrets very much that she was not able to per-suade the other patronesses to agree to Sophie's ad-mittance. The letter sounds as if she is sincerely sorry," added Lady Corby, turning to Sophie. "I am sorry, too, my dear. I had hoped her patronage would be sufficient, but I'm afraid it was not."

"Nonsense!" exclaimed Sir John, jumping to his feet in a rage. "That woman's supposed to be the queen of society. Let me see that letter." He took it quickly from Lady Corby's outstretched hand and pe-rused it rapidly. Sophie was experiencing a full range of emotions, from relief to a surprising degree of dis-appointment. She had not realized how much she had looked forward to the assemblies as an answer to the tedium of her restricted life. Having finished the let-ter, her father said in disgusted tones, " 'Regrets,' fid-dle! I imagine she just didn't want to put herself out. Damned Whig!"

"Am I interrupting something?" asked a familiar voice. Sophie, who had been watching her father, turned quickly to find Tony standing with his customary air of ease in the open doorway. His expression was one of polite concern, but Sophie detected a suppressed smile that told her Sir John's last remark had not gone unheard. But glad as she was to see him, Sophie regretted his bad timing and winced at the irritated expression that had instantly appeared on her father's face.

Smothering the retort he truly wished to make, Sir John managed a curt welcome. "Oh, it is you, sir, is it?" he growled. "You are, perhaps, catching us at a bad time. We have just received some rather unwelcome tidings and will have to discuss how best to deal with the matter." His tone was not inviting.

But Tony, seemingly insensitive to undercurrents, entered the room, anyway.

"I am sorry to hear that, Sir John," he said. "Is there anything I can do to be of service?"

Sir John's irritation escaped its bounds, and he let forth a loud snort, "That is not very likely, sir. If my influence is not enough to get Sophia into Almack's— after years of hunting the Quorn with Hugo Meynell's pack—then I don't think anyone's is. Why, I shall never forget following Lord Jersey's lead when he and Cecil Forester, as he then was, rode right up to the hounds and took their fences flying." Sir John momentarily forgot the issue at hand in appreciation of the remembrance. His frown of irritation faded, and he winked at Tony with the knowledge of an insider.

"Mind you," he said confidentially, "Meynell was not at all pleased with their form of hunting. Called it 'their racing ideas.' But he couldn't do it, you see. He rode too heavily and wasn't up to the jumps. I half-suspect it was the change in form that led him to give up the pack. Said he hadn't enjoyed a moment of the hunt since it became the thing." Sir John shook his head sympathetically.

"But you were not of the same mind I take it?" said Tony, quite willing to help Sir John out of his bad temper.

He was rewarded by a chuckle. "No, not I," admitted Sophie's father. "But I was a much younger man than Meynell, you see. And that sort of daring was very appealing to me. Now, of course, everybody hunts that way. Adds challenge to the sport."

"I can see that it would," agreed Tony.

It was an ill-judged comment, for it served to remind Sir John to whom he was speaking. And that led instantly to the matter of Lady Jersey's note.

Frowning once again, Sir John turned back to the message he was holding and slapped the paper with the back of one hand. "And this is the return I get for going against Hugo Meynell, it seems. Lady Jersey does not see her way to admitting my daughter to Almack's. That is what comes of hunting with Whigs and the like. I suppose I have been well served." He tossed the letter down on a table and walked back to his seat, taking up a newspaper to avoid conversing further with Tony.

Lady Corby rushed in to make up for her husband's lack of courtesy. "Won't you sit down, Sir Tony," she said. "I apologize for your finding us in this dismal state, but, you see, we had quite hoped that Sophia would be admitted. It is rather disappointing."

Tony's expression, which had held a grin at Sir John's last remark, softened at his hostess's gentle voice. "Please do not think of it, Lady Corby. I am as disappointed for you as I am for myself, for I had hoped for a chance to stand up with Miss Corby at the assemblies." He turned to Sophie with a questioning smile.

"Did you truly wish to be admitted, Miss Corby?"

Sophie was surprised at the degree of understanding in his eyes. It was as if he were privy to all her fears and doubts, and she remembered his own confession about not wanting to belong to the Four-Horse Club. But his previous remark, about having wanted to dance with her, awoke in her a strong feeling of regret. If Tony had the habit of going to the assemblies, then she need not have feared attending them. Just knowing there was someone in the ballroom who seemed to have her welfare in mind, someone, moreover, who was at home in any situation, would have been enough to ensure her enjoyment. Right now he was taking her outstretched hand in greeting.

"Yes," said Sophie, in belated answer to his question. "I should have liked to be admitted."

Tony's smile held a special significance. Speaking in a lowered voice, as if for her benefit alone, he said, "Then we shall see what can be done about it." And he winked at her before releasing her hand and turning to speak to Lady Corby.

The two ladies and Tony conversed pleasantly for a while despite Sir John's retreat behind his newspaper, but before long, Tony judged the time was right to withdraw. He had just begun to rise to his feet to take leave of them when Sir John leapt to his with a startled oath.

"Good Gad!" he cried as their eyes turned to him. "This is intolerable!" His face was alarmingly red; his eyes were bulging.

"What is the matter, Sir John?" asked Lady Corby, with less concern than might have been expected under the circumstances. Her relative calm was enough to assure Tony that she must be used to such outbursts.

"This article!" he answered, slapping the paper with a gesture that even Tony, in their limited acquaintance, was coming to know. "I never thought I would live to see the day that such a shocking practice would be discussed in my newspaper. Why the very thought of it makes me shudder, and yet here is this fool discussing it as if the matter were open to question!"

"What matter, dear?" asked Lady Corby patiently.

Sir John could barely bring himself to articulate it. He was visibly shaken. "It is the practice of using live bait for fishing," he said with disgust. "This—this fool," he said, striking the paper again, "has the nerve to write about it and ask whether it might not be a more successful method. Successful! Why, aside from the obvious horror, the simple poor sportsmanship of it is astounding!"

Familiar as she was with her father's thoughts on this issue, Sophie herself had very little opinion on the matter. It had always puzzled her that Sir John should draw a distinction between dangling a live animal of the lowest order before a fish and allowing the hounds to tear a fox to shreds. But now she had to suppress a giggle when she saw the amusement in the glance Tony threw her. And her gravity was maintained with even greater difficulty when Tony bounded to his feet.

"Shocking, indeed, Sir John!" he agreed emphatically. "I am surprised to see such unethical reporting in a respected newspaper. You will no doubt wish to send a stinging admonishment to the editor."

"That I will, by Gad!" said Sir John, no less outraged, but happy to have a vent for his displeasure. "I shall inform him that I do not intend to continue reading a sheet which gives space to such infamous drivel."

"That ought certainly to give them pause," agreed Tony. "I would be honoured to add my name to your letter. But now," said he, turning to the ladies with a calmer tone of voice, "I must take my leave of you.

There is a matter of business I must attend to.'' He
smiled at them both, but Sophie fancied his eyes lin-
gered on her as he made his farewell. Sir John bade him
goodbye absently. He was already composing his letter to the editor.

There were no other happenings of note that day or
the next. But on the third day after Tony's call, Lady
Corby received another note from Lady Jersey. This
time it was to the effect that Sophie's name had been
raised once again before the patronesses at Almack's
and no objections had been forthcoming. The letter
was accompanied by applications for vouchers.

Sir John and Lady Corby were agreed that the previous letter had simply been a mistake and that Sir
John's acquaintance with Lord Jersey had finally been
enough to sway the ruling ladies. Sir John forgot his
grievance against Whigs enough to declare Lady Jersey a valuable ally. But Sophie suspected that Tony
might have had something to do with her acceptance,
for she had neither forgotten his smile nor his wink.
The wink, in fact, came often to mind, and she found
it just as attractive as the first.

The next Wednesday night then, Sophie made her
appearance at the assembly rooms at Almack's clad in
a becoming off-white high-waisted muslin gown. The
peachy colour of her cheeks was complemented by the
saffron-coloured ribbons in her brown hair, and her
large eyes shone with excitement. Searching the room
for faces she knew, she was dazzled by the glow of the

candles and the magnificence of the array of dancers. Lady Jersey greeted them grandly, and they were able to give her their thanks for her efforts on Sophie's behalf.

Before long, Sophie's hand was claimed for a dance, and she was out on the ballroom floor. Although her partner was unknown to her, she still enjoyed the experience of dancing, for in truth, Sophie was not shy. She had simply never been in a large company where her interest did not quickly fade, but the novelty of her surroundings was enough tonight to keep her eyes dancing brightly.

The set came to a close, and a gentleman appeared at her side to request her hand for the next. It was Tony. His eyes swept her from head to toe with an admiring glance, and he bowed to her with an unusual flourish, but Sophie felt the compliment behind the gesture. Although she had been pleased with her own appearance when she had examined herself in the glass, the splendour of those around her, not confined to the simple dress of the ingenue, had given her doubts. Now, with his obvious approval, she dimpled attractively.

"Permit me to say how delighted I am to see you here this evening, Miss Corby," said Tony, offering his arm. "I hope your father is recovered from his attack of the other day?"

She looked at him impishly and replied, "You must not mind Papa. He is frequently given to attacks when a question of good sportsmanship comes up. Live bait is one of his particular dislikes."

"Rightly so!" agreed Tony with a twinkle. "I hope he has written his letter to the editor. I had half a mind to call the fellow out myself!"

Sophie smiled, but her eyes widened. "I am so glad you did not make that suggestion to Papa, for he might have taken it seriously."

Tony leaned a bit closer to speak in a confidential tone, and Sophie was suddenly aware of his essence. "I confess the thought did occur to me," he said, "but I was afraid he might take it up and offer to be my second. Duels are not much in my line, you know."

They had now entered a set, and they took their places before Sophie addressed him again with a shrewd eye out for a change in his expression.

"Are you not surprised to see me, Sir Tony? I believe you were present when we received a disappointing note from Lady Jersey?"

His expression was all innocence. "Yes, I am. Surprised and delighted, as I said."

"And yet," she said, regarding him quizzically, "I think you had more to do with my attending than you would have me think, Sir Tony. How did you manage to change their minds?"

"It was only one mind," he said, not bothering to deny it. "I would not have you think that there was more than one vote against you. You see, most of the patronesses at Almack's can be reasonably applied to, and certainly would not vote against someone approved by one of their members, but the Countess Lieven sometimes requires persuasion.''

"The wife of the Russian ambassador?" asked Sophie.

"The same," said Tony, drawing near her again to speak in a low voice. "The countess is convinced that where *she* is, *there* is fashionable society, and she rather delights in passing judgement on us all, I fancy. It gives her a feeling of superiority, something her aristocratic Russian soul cannot do without. But she had nothing against you personally.'' He seemed inclined to end his explanation there.

But Sophie's curiosity had not been satisfied. Even though she could not be called au courant with the London ton, given the limits of her parents' acquaintance, still she had heard rumours about the Countess Lieven. That lady was new enough to London and had made sufficient sensation that everyone had something to say about her. And it was rumoured that her affairs were numerous. Remembering the Cyprians in the park and their inexplicable familiarity with Sir Tony, Sophie had a peculiarly anxious moment. Just what was his influence with the ambassadress?

In a tone that was as light as she could possibly make it, she asked him more pointedly, "What was it that you said to convince her, then, Sir Tony? I hope you are placed under no obligation to her on my account.''

She did not know that her expression gave away the nature of her concerns.

Tony glanced down at her as they joined hands and moved to the end of the set. His lips were curved in unmistakable enjoyment, but he had to wait to answer her for they were separated in the pattern of the dance and did not come back together for many minutes. During this time, Sophie threw him furtive glances, while trying not to lose her way in the dance. The unanswered question disturbed her tranquility sufficiently to make concentration on the pattern difficult, but Tony showed no such discomfort. She saw that he was moving gracefully through the set with his accustomed ease. Remembering suddenly the bolting horses in the park and Tony's loss of composure on that occasion, Sophie was reassured and was able to greet him with a more trusting smile when next they came together.

Her restored confidence may have eliminated any intention of Tony's to tease her, for he replied to her question with the same honesty with which he had spoken earlier.

"Political intrigue," he said confidentially, "is the Countess Lieven's specialty. I'm afraid I used a rather underhanded trick upon the lady, quite unlike me, but I seem to be strangely motivated of late." He looked at Sophie with a curious lift of his eyebrows, and she coloured without reason. He continued, "I told the Countess a political secret that she has been hoping to learn. She was most grateful and willingly repaid me by sponsoring your name to Almack's.''

Sophie's eyes widened in horror. "But, Sir Tony!" she cried. "I would not have you do such a thing for me! Why, I had much rather not be admitted!" She was dismayed to think that, in her inexperience, she might have misunderstood this man.

But Tony smiled reassuringly and squeezed the hand laid so lightly in his. "Miss Corby, you may rest assured that I would never do anything in the least dishonourable, certainly not attached to your name. The secret I gave her is no longer a secret. It will appear in the papers tomorrow. By now, even the Countess has learned that it is common street gossip which will be confirmed tomorrow by the government.''

Sophie's relief was so strong that she sighed as she gave a laugh. "But will you not lose your goodwill with the Countess now that she knows?''

Tony shook his head confidently. "I do not think so. As I made it appear, the knowledge came to me through a member of the government, and as far as the Countess knows, I was as ignorant of its becoming public as she was.'' He looked at her and winked conspiratorially. "That was the genius of the plan.''

Sophie again laughed happily. A wave of elation had filled her. It was wonderful how Tony could make her feel, somehow, more in the know than those in the know. He could laugh without malice at those who laughed with malice. And he made her feel as open, free and at ease as he always seemed to be.

The dance ended soon, and Sophie reluctantly turned to find that her next partner was to be Mr. Rollo. On this occasion he was willing to give her his full attention, and so, not begging an introduction to her previous partner, led her back into the dance. Mr. Rollo, too, exhibited considerable skill on the dance floor, but somehow he lacked the easy delivery of Tony's performance. There was a studied air to Mr. Rollo's dancing, almost as though he were certain of being watched.

"You handle the steps beautifully, Miss Corby," he said, and Sophie resisted the impulse to return the compliment in the pause that ensued. "One would say that you had been here many times before, instead of its being your first assembly."

Sophie smiled politely, but preferred to direct the conversation away from herself. "Have you been a member for many seasons now, Mr. Rollo?" she asked.

Condescendingly, he replied, "Indeed, yes. But that must not discomfit you in any way. You will find the society here overwhelming at first, I know, but you must not consider your place in it in any way inferior to those with more experience of Town life. With time, you, too, will have the same confidence."

Sophie thanked him as they parted in the set, but she stifled a grimace of distaste as she turned away. In truth, she was finding Mr. Rollo's conversation to be unreasonably centred upon himself and his opinion thereof. She had not been thinking herself inferior to the company in any way, merely different. And that, she trusted, would always be true.

She had no trouble attending to her dance steps in this set, and the time passed quickly until she was reunited with her partner.

"It has occurred to me, Miss Corby," Mr. Rollo said after a well-executed bow, "that my experience in society might be of some use to you in these rather awesome circumstances. I fear that the quiz, to which everyone is subject upon entering, may have been disconcerting to one only recently out of the schoolroom, such as yourself, and perhaps I may be of service." He grimaced smugly. "You must first realize that you have been accepted by one of the most exclusive assemblies in the world. Here you will meet with princes and princesses, lords and ladies—and these, too, I must remind you, have had to apply for the approval of the patronesses no less than yourself—and among them, many sirs and the select misters that make up the best that society has. You have, in short, passed the scrutiny at Almack's, and having done that, need have no further worries of acceptance by the elite." He finished and waited for Sophie's gratitude to be dutifully expressed.

She complied as reasonably as politeness would allow, but Mr. Rollo was not unduly disappointed. He was mentally disposed to fill in wherever her own thanks should be deficient.

With token confidence in her abilities, then, he offered, "I will not presume to overwhelm you with advice, Miss Corby. Your own good sense will tell you how to go on." Somehow his superior smile did not convey the same confidence as his words.

Sophie was grateful for a change of partners when the dance ended. She was not obliged to take a rest from the dancing, for her hand was claimed for every set. Mr. Rollo returned later in the evening to beg for another, and this time he reminded her that the date for their proposed visit to the Royal Academy was approaching. She acknowledged the truth of it, but privately found that she was not looking forward to the scheme with the same degree of delight she had felt earlier. Her partner, however, was certain of the pleasure she would derive from it and spent the remainder of the time they were together in telling her of the treat that was in store.

As he took his departure with a solemn bow, Sophie became aware that Tony was waiting to claim the next dance. Immediately, though the length of the evening had become rather oppressive, her spirits rose.

"Are you enjoying the assembly, Miss Corby?" he asked, and she fancied he wished for an honest answer.

"Yes," she said without affectation, but then added with a haughty look, "having now passed the scrutiny of this august assembly, I need not be concerned that my qualifications to take place among the elite will be questioned further." She was pleased to see him start and turn to look at her closely. Her impish smile reassured him, and he answered with a twinkle.

"Indeed, they will not. I suppose some bore has been telling you so, in case it were not perfectly clear. You have had no small number of partners this evening, and I will not be so rude as to ask you which one has such an elevated opinion of himself." Sophie smothered a giggle.

"Do you think," she asked, after a moment's pause, "that in my advanced years *I* shall be quizzing young ladies and gentlemen as they enter these portals? Ought I to cultivate a certain look, a lifted eyebrow, a faint sneer to set their knees a-trembling? Would it advance my own position within the ton?"

Tony grinned. "No. Leave that for the elite masses. You must remain just as you are."

"But can I?" asked Sophie, this time more seriously. "If balls and assemblies are to become a habit, even a bore, perhaps, shall I always be the same?"

"I think so," he answered unconcernedly. "These amusements never lose their essential qualities. It is only when the security of one's position becomes more important than simply enjoying oneself that one stops enjoying society. And then, of course, you must do things to fight for that position, always at the cost of someone else's. But you will not do that." He smiled at her in a way that warmed her heart.

She coloured and strived to cover up how much he had affected her. "Then I needn't quiz anyone?" she asked, lightly this time.

"No."

She sighed resignedly. "I had rather looked forward to quizzing someone, but if you insist . . ." Her voice trailed off, and he grinned as they moved apart.

The dance was a lively reel and did not permit much conversation, but once again they were together long enough for Tony to ask, "Who was that gentleman, Miss Corby, whom you danced with earlier?" His voice was uncharacteristically indifferent. "I fancied it was he who claimed your hand after our first dance."

"Oh, that was Mr. Rollo," answered Sophie matter-of-factly. "He is a friend of Papa's."

Tony nodded, "Ah, I see. You must see him often in Berkeley Square, then." His eyebrow lifted slightly.

"Yes, we do," said Sophie with a forced gaiety. She thought it her duty to sound cheerful about her father's choice of company. "As a matter of fact, Mr. Rollo has kindly invited me to go with him to see the Royal Academy. Of course, I shall be delighted," she said, reflecting that her delight lay in the promise of a new attraction rather than in the company.

"Of course," said Tony, sounding slightly less than delighted himself. "What day would you be going?"

"On Friday," said Sophie with some surprise. "Why do you ask?"

Tony responded quite innocently. "Why, simply because I am engaged to do the same, and coincidentally, on the same day. And you think you will be going at . . . ?" He left off expectantly.

"At two o'clock" was the answer.

The corners of his mouth turned up approvingly. "Excellent," he said. "The very best time of day to go. That was when I had intended going myself."

CHAPTER SIX

UNBEKNOWNST TO SOPHIE, a change of plans had been made concerning the trip to the Royal Academy. Mr. Rollo had informed Sir John that two of his friends had begged to be included in the scheme, and Sophie's father had then suggested to Lady Corby that she stay at home. The young people would have more fun without her along, he had said. They would get to know each other better.

And in reply to Lady Corby's disappointment at not seeing the Academy, he had promised to take her there himself at a future date, with no intention, of course, of ever keeping it. Lady Corby was not deceived. Her married life was full of such unkept promises, though she did not accuse Sir John of purposefully lying to her, merely of putting off into an obscure future all the things he did not truly wish to do.

Friday afternoon arrived, and Mr. Rollo appeared at the door; his two friends were waiting in the carriage. Sophie had only been apprised of the change in plans that morning and was not terribly pleased to find that the "two friends" could have been more accurately termed "a pair." The young lady and gentleman were seated in the rear seat of the phaeton with, it seemed, no more than an inch between them, and her arm was rather permanently linked through his. Mr. Rollo introduced them as Miss Kate Stanfield and Mr. Repton. They greeted her politely and then returned to their whisperings with an occasional giggle or squeal from Miss Stanfield.

Mr. Rollo handed Sophie into the carriage, and she took her seat as far from the centre as safety would allow. She hoped that no one would see them and draw conclusions about the two in front based upon the behaviour of the pair in back. Being in this quartet made her feel uncomfortably particular, much more so than had riding alone with Sir Tony.

Mr. Rollo's team of horses consisted of four beautifully matched bays. They were showy and obviously well cared for, so Sophie felt safe in opening the conversation with a comment on their excellence. She could not have picked a better topic.

"Thank you, Miss Corby," Mr. Rollo replied, beaming. "I do not deny that they are a fine team. They were purchased directly from Lord Pipcock at a considerable price and only after what must be considered the most fortunate occurrence. You will scarcely credit my good luck. He had just lost his entire fortune at cards the night before and was quite desperate to raise enough funds to flee the country—

otherwise he would not have parted with them." Mr. Rollo's tone solicited her warmest congratulations.

"*You*, indeed, were most fortunate, Mr. Rollo," said Sophie with the slightest emphasis.

"Yes, wasn't I?" said Rollo, but not without a hint of meriting it fully. "And I have not been disappointed with them. Of course, I would give my ancestral home to have a team of matched greys, but to come in the way of purchasing such a team as this is not every man's good fortune. Repton and I have been trying them at their full pace between Sevenoaks and Maidstone, and we are confident that they've tied the record. Isn't that so, Repton?" he called back to the rear seat for confirmation.

But all he got by way of reply were some muffled words and a giggle from the back seat. Mr. Rollo shrugged his shoulders with a smirk in their direction and offered this explanation to Sophie, "Do not mind them, Miss Corby. They are newly engaged to be married. I can only congratulate my friend Repton upon finding the right lady to complement his household. I hope to see myself as well-connected one day soon." This last was said with a look of confidence in Sophie's direction.

Sophie hastened to change the subject and was able to persuade Mr. Rollo to continue speaking about his horses. But he managed to flatter her once more.

"I was certain to find in you an excellent judge of horses, Miss Corby. As knowledgeable as your father is, you must often hear him speak of them."

She hastened to deny it. "Oh, you are quite mistaken, Mr. Rollo. Indeed, I know very little about horses. Only how to ride them. And I must add that I do not perform that very well."

"Well, no matter," said Rollo, evidently not in the least put off. "I would not expect a lady to show much expertise in the matter of horseflesh. It is enough that your father is so notable a judge."

Sophie was not certain of the intention of his last statement and not at all clear how it related to Mr. Rollo's approval of herself. But she went on, hoping to discourage him somehow. "My father would not consider himself an expert on coach horses, sir. Aside from a few episodes during his days at university, he has never shown an interest in becoming a coachman."

Mr. Rollo became instantly more serious. He leaned toward her slightly and spoke earnestly. "Ah, Miss Corby," he said with a sigh. "How I envy him that choice. Had I a domicile in Leicestershire or the means of maintaining myself and my horses for the season in Melton Mowbray, I should not be occupying myself in this fashion. I can sincerely assure you that once I have achieved a more permanent residence in that blessed county, I shall abandon all my less important pursuits. No man, when given the opportunity, would choose differently." He sighed so heavily that Sophie, had she had any inclination to disbelieve him, would have reversed it.

But she did not doubt his words. They only confirmed what she had suspected of him from their first acquaintance. And now it was clear to her that Mr. Rollo intended to use her to obtain his heart's desire. That was the reason that it mattered not whether they shared the same devotion to the finer points of a horse's conformation. What should it matter so long as her father did? It was her father who could convey that "more permanent residence" in the Shires, and he who was the companion of Mr. Rollo's soul, not his daughter.

They rode on to the Academy in mutual silence, Sophie in serious contemplation of the difficulties she now foresaw, and Rollo in silent longing for his elusive objective.

Sophie was relieved to see when they arrived that Miss Stanfield and Mr. Repton were not so lost to their surroundings that they could not behave with propriety once they were outside the carriage. They linked arms and followed Mr. Rollo as he led the way into Somerset House with Sophie at his side.

There was quite a handsome crowd assembled to view the exhibition of pictures, so many in fact that at first Sophie was only aware of the array of bonnets and beavers adorning their heads. But as her eyes grew accustomed to the room, she could see beyond their hats to the immense canvases that adorned the walls, all in elaborate frames. Gentlemen in heroic poses and ladies reclining on sofas looked down upon the crowd, while angelic children, often on the backs of ponies or seated with a pet dog in their laps, raised their eyes heavenward. She was so pleased with the general effect that she had to smile at Mr. Rollo, who was awaiting her reaction.

"A splendid scene, is it not, Miss Corby? I come here often to enjoy it. And a mere shilling's admittance is no hindrance. It only serves to assure one of the respectability of all others present. You will discover that there are many astute critics among the crowd, and you have only to overhear their comments to benefit from their judgement. After three or perhaps four visits, you will begin to form judgements for yourself and be better able to assess the progress of a new artist in the improvement of his work."

Sophie inclined her head in acceptance of his assessment, for she was quite willing to believe herself incapable of an educated opinion on the artists. She had never had the chance to observe so many fine works of art, no one in her own family having the slightest inclination to obtain any. So taking Mr. Rollo's proffered arm, she prepared to enjoy the next hour.

They obtained a list of the portraits that were hung in the many rooms and strolled through the thick crowd to admire them. Mr. Rollo commented on each for her benefit, not neglecting to tell her the price most recently fetched by each artist on his piece in the previous competition. She noticed that Mr. Rollo's opinion of each of the present works was either high or low in direct correlation with the sum now offered for that artist's work.

"A splendid execution!" he would assert before a portrait of strictly formal composition. "I should not be at all surprised if this portrait places quite high in the competition."

"Indeed, Mr. Rollo?" ventured Sophie. "I do not see that it distinguishes itself in any way from the other, though, of course, it is quite pleasing."

He turned toward her with a superior smile. "You would not, Miss Corby," he assured her. "This is merely your first visit to Somerset House and you cannot expect to be as discerning on such limited knowledge. But I can inform you that this same artist was the clear winner in the previous competition and this is not inferior to his last work. You would not credit the price that was fetched on that occasion, I daresay."

"Perhaps not, Mr. Rollo," agreed Sophie abashed. They moved on to the next portrait, but Sophie was startled to hear his next comment.

"What a fetching bonnet!" As the portrait before them pictured a gentleman seated at his desk, Sophie was obliged to look up at Mr. Rollo to find the reason behind his remark. It then became obvious that his eyes had wandered and had located an object of greater interest nearby. A lady and a gentleman were seated together on an elegant bench in the middle of the room and were comparing comments on a picture placed on the opposite wall. The lady's bonnet was quite elegant, and Sophie agreed pleasantly before returning to gaze silently at the gentleman's portrait before her.

They proceeded through the room slowly, Mr. Rollo occasionally making an instructional remark about a painting, but just as often commenting upon the appearance of or his acquaintance with someone in the gallery. The engaged pair followed in their wake, taking perhaps less notice of the splendour on the wall before them. Suddenly, however, Sophie's attention was claimed by a startled oath coming from Mr. Rollo himself.

"Good Gad!" he exclaimed. "What a shocking daub!" He spoke with an emotion he had not heretofore shown.

They had arrived before a handsome portrait. The subject was a noble duke, well known for the excellence of his hunting pack. He was seated upon a magnificent steed, his red jacket proclaiming his Tory politics. And at his horse's feet were gathered a number of elegantly drawn hounds.

Sophie turned to Mr. Rollo in some surprise, but before she could ask him what he found so shocking about a picture she would have expected him to find particularly pleasing, a voice spoke over her shoulder.

"Oh, really? I rather like it myself." Sophie spun around, and Mr. Rollo was obliged to release her arm to discover who had addressed him so impudently, for the voice came clearly between them. Sir Tony was standing, regarding the painting, his face the perfect picture of self-doubt. He smiled at Mr. Rollo in his open, friendly fashion, then turned to address Sophie.

"Your servant, Miss Corby," he said, tipping his beaver.

"Good afternoon," she said, dimpling. Sophie felt herself relaxing immediately in his presence, realizing only then what an effort it had been to hold a conversation with Mr. Rollo.

"An acquaintance of yours, Miss Corby?" that young man now enquired.

Sophie started. "Oh, yes. Pray excuse me, Mr. Rollo. May I make you known to Sir Tony Farnham?"

"Farnham?" said Rollo brightening visibly. He had been about to take exception to the interruption, but could not do so before a connection he was pleased to make.

"Delighted to meet you, sir. I have heard much about your skill with the ribbons and have hoped for such a meeting. I'm told you made the run from Brighton to Newhaven in just under thirty minutes."

"I'm afraid that report was much exaggerated," said Tony, politely dismissing the subject. "I never time my own journeys. Are you enjoying the exhibition, Miss Corby?" he asked with a smile.

Sophie started to answer, but Mr. Rollo ignored Tony's last remark and pursued his own line of thought. "But I understand that Lord Whitpenny was with you and that he clocked your time."

Tony turned his gaze upon Mr. Rollo; the smile on his face was becoming rather fixed. "Yes, Whitpenny was with me, but I did not ask him to time the journey and have little interest in knowing it. I was merely testing my new team of horses, letting them have their heads, as it were." He attempted to speak to Sophie again, but was prevented once more by Mr. Rollo's persistence.

"Oh, no!" said that young man with a hearty laugh. "Not interested are you? But you managed to have a member of the Four-in-Hand Club along!" He laughed again and gave Tony a slap on the back rather suggestive of complicity.

Tony's smile became strained, but he declined to respond and instead looked at Sophie expectantly.

"Yes," she said in answer to his earlier question. "I am enjoying it excessively. I have never seen so many lovely pictures."

"It is rather impressive, is it not?" said Tony. "How fortunate I was to run into you." He perceived that Mr. Rollo was about to ask him another question about his coaching reputation, so he cut him off with a reminder about the portrait before them. "I believe I interrupted you, Mr. Rollo, when you were about to explain your objections to this painting. Pray continue."

Tony's words recalled to Rollo's mind the grievous offence of the artist in question, and he turned to it immediately with a frown. "Ah, yes. Shocking! But I do not need to point out its fault to a sporting gentleman like yourself, Sir Tony. Nor to Miss Corby with her practiced eye."

Sophie, widening her big, brown eyes in surprise, denied any knowledge of the painting's fault. Tony also answered in the negative, explaining that if the fault lay in the execution of the painting, he could not find it.

Rollo looked at them both with an incredulous expression. It was almost as if he suspected them of trying to gammon him.

"It's the hounds!" he exclaimed. "They are all wrong! Surely, you can see that, Miss Corby?" Sophie looked once more at the portrait and again denied it. Rollo was aghast. "Look at their legs," he hinted. Sophie and Tony both did so, but their empty expressions gave him no satisfaction. Finally Rollo gave up and made all clear to them. "You surely must see that they are too long. His grace's pack is all short-legged with well muscled forelegs."

"Really!" exclaimed Tony, suitably impressed. "I should never have noticed it. Remarkable, don't you think, Miss Corby?"

Sophie suppressed a laugh. "Most certainly," she agreed.

Rollo was pleased to have impressed them both on such an important point. "Shocking, isn't it?" he repeated. "It puzzles me why his grace allowed the thing to be shown."

"Yes," Tony nodded. "It is a mystery. But I happen to know his grace, and the picture really is quite good of *him*. The stirrup leather seems an appropriate length." Sophie put a hand suddenly over her mouth and coughed.

After a quick glance in her direction, Tony changed the subject. He looked about the room as if searching for someone and then remarked, "Oh, dear me. I seem to have become separated from my friends. They are nowhere in sight." He avoided Sophie's suspicious look and turned to Mr. Rollo instead. "Perhaps you would not mind if I joined you temporarily." He smiled ingenuously.

"Not at all, dear fellow," said Mr. Rollo sincerely. "We should be delighted."

"Thank you, sir," said Tony with a slight bow. He then offered his arm to Sophie. "Miss Corby?" She took it with no more than a dimple betraying her understanding of how Tony had outmanoeuvred Mr. Rollo, and they proceeded to the next picture with Rollo following along behind. Miss Stanfield and Mr. Repton, who had taken no part in the previous conversation, were now trailing by only a few paces.

They caught up with the others and were presented to Sir Tony, who greeted them with his customary courtesy. They then admired the picture, which again was a hunting portrait. In acknowledgement of Rollo's superior knowledge on the subject, Tony begged him to elucidate it for them. Nothing loath, Rollo complied and was gratified when Tony posed a quantity of questions about the horse's conformation, the hounds, the weight of the rider, the excellence of the pack and the accuracy of the artist's rendition. But to Sophie, the questions seemed to be endless, and, as her mind drifted away from the scene before her, she wondered if this was merely Tony's way of learning about something which newly fascinated him.

Before too long, Mr. Repton was drawn into the conversation, and it became clear that he, too, was a hunting enthusiast. He offered his opinion as freely as did Mr. Rollo, until inevitably they disagreed upon something which had very little to do with the painting at all. Repton's father, it seemed, owned a pack of harriers and saw no harm, therefore, in entering hounds to hare before they were entered to fox. Mr. Rollo disagreed and argued strongly that it was an outmoded practice which experience had shown to be wrong. They argued more and more hotly, each keeping a tenuous hold on a veneer of polite disagreement, while Tony, Sophie and Miss Stanfield looked on. The latter young lady was still on her fiancé's arm and had to listen to the growing argument with no recourse.

But, not so Tony and Sophie. They distanced themselves a bit when Tony stepped back into the crowd, ostensibly to permit another group of viewers to approach the painting, and drew Sophie with him. As they were now no longer a part of the quarrelling group, they were free to pursue their own conversation.

"We seem to be cut off from our friends for the moment, Miss Corby. Perhaps you would take a minute to let me show you a painting that I spotted earlier in the afternoon," he suggested hopefully.

Sophie wanted to go, but her conscience troubled her. "I would be happy to see it, Sir Tony, but perhaps I should ask the others to come with us. I would not want them to think I was unwilling to wait for them." She looked back toward her companions, but the two gentlemen were still hotly debating their point, and even Miss Stanfield had not seemed to notice that Sophie and Tony were no longer with them.

Tony spoke encouragingly. "I should not worry too much over it, Miss Corby. They seem to be perfectly happy at the moment, and I should think that the discussion could go on for a minute or two longer. The painting is just a little ways away." He smiled at her, and she felt the irresistible pull of his blue eyes.

"Very well, then." They stepped across the room to a wall she had not seen and stopped before a rather smallish painting. It was of a young lady, dressed for a country walk, but without a bonnet. She was seated on a rustic stile, a sheaf of papers in her lap, a pen in her hand, and she was gazing off into the distance lost in thought. Sophie looked at the picture for a long moment, while Tony watched her. Then she flushed with pleasure before commenting simply, "I like it."

"I had hoped you would," he said. "As soon as I saw it, I thought of you and how you must often go on solitary walks to think and to write. Am I correct?"

"Yes," she admitted shyly. No one had ever asked about her solitary rambles.

"I knew it," said Tony quietly. "The artist could have known you."

"Indeed?" teased Sophie, now amused. "Is it very like?" And thinking of Mr. Rollo's critical comments, she added, "Perhaps the length of the legs is a bit off." Then suddenly, as the impropriety of her words struck her, she reddened and lowered her gaze.

But Tony answered as though an improper meaning had not occurred to him. "Perhaps it is," he said thoughtfully. Then after a pause, he added seriously, "But I am not yet in a position to be certain."

And seemingly unaware of her blushes, he began to comment on the pleasant colours in the canvas and the artist's visible brush stroke, until Sophie remembered the others.

"Sir Tony," she reminded him. "I think we ought to be returning to my companions. They must have finished their discussion by now and might be searching for me."

"Let us hope so," said Tony seriously. "They really ought not to have entered into a disagreement in front of their guests, and I would not be in the least surprised if Mr. Rollo is not regretting his error now."

"But wasn't it you, Sir Tony, who brought up the issue of entering fox hounds to hare when Mr. Repton mentioned his father had a pack of harriers?" she reminded him.

"Did I?" asked Tony innocently. "I must have heard the topic discussed before. But," he cautioned her with a twinkle, "you must remind me never to mention it again."

CHAPTER SEVEN

THE FOURTEENTH OF APRIL was Sophie's birthday, and her mother planned to give a small dinner party in her honour. Cards were sent out to a select group of friends among whom were included Sir Tony and Mr. Rollo.

Aunt Sadie, who had spent most of the past month on her property in Kent, planned to return to Town for the birthday party and remain for the rest of the social season. Now that warmer weather could be expected, she would not be plagued by the twinges in her injured back which often curtailed her enjoyment of Town pleasures. Sophie, who had never seen her aunt in the least inhibited by these twinges, still knew that they must be considerable if they kept Sadie from the chase, for only a major discomfort could have done so.

On the evening of the Corbys' dinner party, Aunt Sadie was the first to arrive by prearrangement. It was with a mixture of curiosity and dread that all the Corbys looked forward to hearing her comments about Sophie's social successes to date. They were not all agreed, however, on which success was the most promising for her future settlement in life.

After the initial considerable bustle which typically accompanied Aunt Sadie's entry into any house, they moved to the parlour to await the arrival of their guests. Sophie was dressed in a lovely, sprig-yellow gown. Her mother and she were both agreed that the stark white of the debutante did not become her peach-coloured complexion, but this bright yellow seemed to enhance the glow in her smooth cheeks and the gleam in her brown eyes. Aunt Sadie looked her over with proud approval.

"You are a beauty, Sophie," she said stoutly. "I always expected you would be. You're like your mother was at the same age. Of course, you wouldn't be getting it from the Corbys, for we never produced one with any looks."

"Come, come now, Sadie," protested Lady Corby politely. "I am certain that you were a handsome young lady. You never lacked for admirers."

"Handsome, yes. Beautiful, no, Clarissa. And there's the difference," Sadie answered. "And my 'admirers' were no more than hunting companions. But I wasn't unhappy, and I know that Mr. Brewster married me more for my ability to beat him in a race than for my face. We suited each other well," she said, ending with a touch of hoarseness in her voice.

"Of course, you did, my dear," said Lady Corby, her gentle heart moved. "I never knew a happier marriage.'' She hugged Sadie impulsively, but that lady shrugged off her sad reminiscences with an embarrassed laugh.

"Let's not get started on that, Clarissa, or we shall spoil Sophie's party. She's already startled to see her Aunt Sadie lapse into the sentimental. Never you mind, dear, I'm not like to weep into my handkerchief and miss talking to all your young men.'' She laughed and seemed fully restored to equanimity.

Sophie was indeed staring, but not because of Sadie's rare tears. She had never questioned the essential tenderness of her aunt's heart. There was another question in her mind, and that was the importance of female beauty to making a happy marriage. It was something she had always been led to believe essential, for her father had frequently thanked his luck for giving him only daughters who had the sense to favour their lovely mother and so, would find it easy to catch husbands.

But Sadie had been truly happy. Much more so than Sophie's mother, despite her beauty. Perhaps, Sophie thought, a marriage with the proper gentleman, one whose enthusiasms matched one's own, was something greatly to be wished.

Sadie's loud laughter had restored the celebratory mood of the occasion, and Lady Corby turned her attention to Sophie, telling her aunt about her daughter's success at the assemblies at Almack's. It came as no surprise to Sadie, though, and she clapped Sophie on the back with such strong approbation that it threatened to undo the carefully achieved row of short curls which circled her niece's head. "Just what I expected," exclaimed Sadie to accompany the gesture. "But what I want to know is if there is any particular beau you fancy."

Sophie was spared answering by her mother who, fearing another blow would seriously damage Sophie's appearance, ushered her sister-in-law to a chair while saying hastily, "It is really too early to tell, Sadie. Although Sophie has been rather distinguished by one or two gentlemen."

"I wouldn't say that, Clarissa," said Sir John with an air of possessing a secret. He had stayed out of the earlier part of the conversation, which had not interested him. "I would say that there is one gentleman, at least, who seems very anxious to make himself agreeable to Sophie." He waited teasingly for his sister to beg him to reveal the name.

But Sadie disappointed him for she turned to Sophie with a knowledgeable smile. "And I'll bet I know who that is. Sir Tony Farnham! Am I right, gel?"

A blush spread quickly over Sophie's cheeks, which could have been considered answer enough, but Sir John recalled Sadie's attention with an angry snort. "Farnham? Nonsense! He is nothing of the sort. I was speaking, if you must know, of a new acquaintance of mine, a Mr. Rollo. A very superior young man. Nothing of the jack o'dandy about him."

"Nor is there about Tony, as I've already told you, John," retorted Sadie. But she showed immediate interest in his pronouncement. "You say that Rollo is hanging out for Sophie, do you? I know the boy. Keeps good company, they say, and there's no denying his talents. Has a good seat and shows exceptional riding skill in the field, I'm told." She glanced at Sophie, but found her niece's face expressionless.

Sir John smiled and gestured to his daughter. "There, Sophie, haven't I been telling you just that."

But his sister's next remark held a note of caution. "I am a bit surprised to hear it, John, nevertheless. I would have expected Rollo to be looking out for a richer wife."

Sir John responded huffily, "Sophie's portion is quite decent enough, Sadie. You should know me better than to think I would not have provided for my own daughter."

"Oh, it's not that, John," she said swiftly. "It is just that I had heard Rollo's estates were in none too good repair. And he does live expensively."

Sir John growled his rejection of the idea. "Nonsense, Sadie. Perhaps you have not heard that the boy stands to inherit a considerable fortune from his aunt. Any day so, in fact, if rumours of her poor health are accurate. I have counselled him against post-obiting, and he accepted my advice with admirable attentiveness. The case cannot be as bad as you say."

Sadie accepted the information reservedly, "In that case, I apologize, John. Perhaps it is not so bad, as you say. I only mention it because I would not want Sophie to find herself without enough blunt for her own comfort."

Sir John was appeased, but he changed the subject with a haste that suggested he was not disposed to delve further into the topic. "No need to fear that, Sadie. Well, at any rate, you will be seeing the boy later. He tells me he has a special surprise for Sophie."

At these words, his daughter squirmed uncomfortably. In fact, the whole previous conversation had distressed her in the extreme. She could not, in all politeness, dispute her father's reading of the situation in front of his sister, but she resolved to try her utmost to convince Sir John privately that she had no particular fondness for Mr. Rollo.

At that moment, however, the first of the guests was announced, and she was kept busy accepting the happy wishes and flowers that the small but continuous stream of visitors brought with them. Tony was among the earliest arrivals, but he carried no flowers with him. However, he did ask for the pleasure of taking her in to dinner. Sophie agreed, happily relieved that Tony had made the request before Mr. Rollo appeared. That young man, however, was the last to arrive, with a confident expectation of welcome which Sophie's father did nothing to belie.

"Ah, there you are, Rollo, my boy," said Sir John heartily. "We had almost given up on you. I understand you are acquainted with my sister, Sarah Brewster."

"Of course," answered Rollo with suave courtesy, "delighted to see you again, Mrs. Brewster. I believe the last time we met was at a race meeting outside Tonbridge Wells. At that time, though, I had no expectation of becoming so happily acquainted with your brother's family."

"I remember," Sadie said, nodding. "You lost rather a handsome purse that day as I recall." She looked up at him quizzically.

"Ah, yes," he said with seemingly little concern. "A mistake in judgement on my part. But even the best of sportsmen are given to occasional errors. I have been more careful in placing my bets since then."

"Excellent boy!" said Sir John. "But we should not keep you talking here. You will want to pay your respects to Sophie. Here she is now." Sophie had stepped forward to greet her new guest as she had done for all the others, but Mr. Rollo took her extended hand with an air of having received a special distinction.

"Miss Corby, my felicitations on this notable occasion. I had scarcely hoped for such a warm welcome in the midst of your friends, except that you are always so particularly generous." Ever at a loss at how to react properly to such unwelcome insinuations, Sophie murmured something unintelligible in reply and was relieved when Tony appeared at her elbow.

"Good day to you, Mr. Rollo," he said heartily. "What a delightful surprise to see you again." His whole face radiated true bonhomie, and the goodwill of his smile completely overcame the unflattering implication of his words. Mr. Rollo was overcome by the distinction.

"Farnham, my dear fellow, the pleasure is all mine," he protested. Then looking Tony over admiringly he added, "I say. I do like the cut of your coat. Who suffers?"

Tony's smile flickered briefly, but then reappeared slightly altered, giving the impression that Mr. Rollo had somehow fulfilled his dearest expectations. "No one," he said bluntly. "You see, Rollo, I *pay* my tailor." He waited for his words to sink in, but his listener took no notice.

"Pay him?" he asked laughing incredulously. "Why, whatever for? Mine will clothe me completely merely for the honour of doing so. He receives considerable business as a result of my mentioning his name, you see. It is a beautiful arrangement. You should try it. Certainly with your sporting reputation you could escape a dun for months at a time."

Sophie thought that Tony's smile was beginning to show signs of strain, but his attention to Mr. Rollo was undiminished. "It is a peculiar particularity of mine, I suppose. I rather like to pay the tradesmen who render me their good service."

Rollo looked momentarily perplexed, but soon a light of comprehension dawned on his face. "Ah, I get it, old fellow. Pay the ones who matter the most. I do that myself. With me, it's my wine merchant. The beggar threatens to cut me off if his bill isn't the first one settled. Most unpleasant, but I cannot afford to do without him. I understand completely." He grimaced sympathetically as he recalled the strident complaints of his wine merchant. Tony grinned broadly, but Sophie noted that his eyes lacked their customary warmth.

Sir John joined them at that moment and reminded Mr. Rollo that he had promised a special surprise for Sophie and that the family was anxiously awaiting his pleasure. That gentleman, recalled to the occasion, smirked at Sophie suggestively and withdrew from his pocket a piece of parchment paper which had been rolled up elegantly and tied with a pink ribbon.

"Ah, yes, Miss Corby. Here it is, as I promised your father. I can see you were just as expectant as he said you would be, and I hope you will not be disappointed in my efforts. It is an ode in honour of your birthday and, if you will permit, I shall read it before the assembled company."

Sophie flushed with annoyance. No one had ever written a poem for her, and certainly no one had ever read one to her in public. She anticipated an uncom-

fortable few minutes, but she could not refuse her
guest's gesture. Nodding her head and thanking Mr.
Rollo politely, she took a chair while her father called
the attention of the others to Mr. Rollo's imminent
performance. Tony took a place behind Sophie's chair
and folded his arms in expectation of some private delight.

The company were soon gathered in a rough semi-
circle about the parlour with Mr. Rollo placed in the
centre. He waited, still smirking, for their voices to die
down and was not at all offended by a shy titter from
an elderly romantic in the audience. Once they were
quieted, he untied the pink ribbon, unrolled the small
parchment and cleared his throat before beginning.

"To Miss Corby, In Honour of Her Birthday," he
read, looking up one last time to assure himself of their
attention. Then he resumed in a more projecting tone.

"'All hail' rings forth this glorious morn' In honour of Miss Corby's nineteenth year. To her I
dedicate this ode, So, pray, my earnest muse to
hear."

Mr. Rollo threw Sophie a glance over the top of his
paper to gauge her reaction to his introduction, man-
aging to include Sir John in its scope. If Sophie's polite smile was not enough to encourage him onward, Sir
John's hearty, "Hear, hear," and vigorous nod of the

head clearly were. Mr. Rollo puffed out his chest and
continued.

> "As gentle Hestia tends the hearth
> For mighty Zeus's Olympian throne,
> So Miss Corby takes her place beside
> The fireplace of her father's home.

> "As Artemis was well endowed
> With Zeus's pack of lop-eared hounds
> So chance has blessed Miss Corby with
> A glorious hunt of world renown."

Mr. Rollo darted a glance at Sir John to measure his
approval, and behind Sophie's chair, Tony emitted a
discreet cough which threatened to disturb her gravity.
But Mr. Rollo returned to his reading, and she lost all
sense of amusement as she listened to the remaining
verses.

> "Fair as Io, warm as Gaea,
> Blessed by Eos' dewy hand,
> All applaud your wondrous beauty
> Among the fairest in the land.

> "Thus, I beseech the playful Cupid,
> Harken to my earnest plea

Release thy shaft on this fair maiden
Win her favour now for me.''

The ode was ended. But to Sophie's intense morti-
fication, as Mr. Rollo reached the end, he looked at her
once again with more than a hint of a suggestion. His
last words could only have one meaning, and this had
not escaped the rest of the company. There was much
applause following the reading of the poem and much
laughter of an approving sort. Sir John, leaping to his
feet at the end, hastened to declare Mr. Rollo's poem
the best birthday ode he had ever heard, as good as the
Poet Laureate's ode to the Queen the previous year, he
was certain. He clapped the young man on the back
and ushered him over to receive Sophie's thanks.

The birthday girl found herself unable to express her
gratitude to Mr. Rollo with any degree of sincerity. She
did not wish to encourage him in his obvious pursuit of
her hand, nor did she want her father to feel encouraged in his misguided matchmaking. She could do no
more than extend her hand as impersonally as possible
under the circumstances and thank him for the kindness of his intentions.

Sir John, however, was not wholly satisfied with this
response. Hoping for something warmer, he prompted
her by saying, ''I told Rollo here about your own poetry, Sophie. And I knew it would please you to have
him write a sonnet to your eyes or some such thing. It
has, hasn't it now?'' His tone did not invite an answer
so much as an affirmation.

But Sophie was spared the difficulty of answering by Tony, who stepped quickly from behind her to shake Mr. Rollo's hand vigorously.

"My dear Rollo, an excellent ode! It puts the rest of us in the shade. I confess I had written my own little something on the occasion, but it pales in the shadow of your composition. I shall not have the courage to read it now. I will not subject myself to ridicule. But may I commend yours," he added obliquely.

Mr. Rollo was beaming from the collective praises of the two gentlemen and did not solicit any more from Miss Corby. Like many sportsmen, he valued the opinion of his peers far more than those of the ladies, believing members of the fair sex to have few firm ideas of their own, anyway. But his well-cultivated good manners prompted him to respond in like fashion, and he begged to hear Tony's poem.

"Yes, you must let us hear it, dear fellow," he persisted when Tony refused. "You must not let my own performance discourage you. You may not realize it, but I am not in the habit of writing poetry and I, at least, shall appreciate your efforts. Devilish tricky!"

Tony's lips twitched, but he did not let on that Mr. Rollo's appreciation would not be the object of his recitation. Instead he drew out of his coat pocket a small parcel neatly done up in paper with a ribbon, saying as he turned toward Sophie, "Thank you, Rollo, but no. I hope that Miss Corby will accept a small birthday gift in place of my own poem, and that she will give me credit for having the sense to yield to a master.'' As he handed her the parcel, his eyes met Sophie's with a look that was suddenly so intense that her own fell before it. She smiled shyly, and Tony watched delightedly as a deep dimple appeared in each cheek. But before Sophie could reply, Mr. Rollo spoke again with strong emotion.

"Dear fellow!" From the number of times he had addressed Tony in this manner, Sophie had to conclude that Tony had become very dear to Mr. Rollo, indeed. "You flatter me beyond words." He seemed overcome by Tony's last remarks and clearly thought them a direct compliment to himself. But Sophie had by now untied the ribbon and unwrapped the thin paper to the parcel, and had found the small book of Shakespeare's sonnets inside. It was a beautifully bound volume with a soft leather backing, deeply set letters and pages edged in gold.

Breathing a gentle "oh," she cradled the book reverently in her hands. Its contents were very familiar to her, but Sophie had never owned such a precious volume. And she now understood the significance of Sir Tony's last words. Looking up to thank him, she was disappointed to find that Mr. Rollo was still claiming his attention. But, she thought, at least she had been able to open it without that gentleman's eyes upon her. She tucked the small book into the folds of her gown, planning to hide it there until she could take a moment to run up to her room.

The two gentlemen's conversation had by now turned to hunting, and Sophie's father had joined in it as a thirsty animal draws near a water hole. Sophie could hear Tony's voice posing an occasional intelligent question, and she smiled, recalling his similar behaviour at the Royal Academy. Promising herself to charge him later with affecting his guileless demeanor and to thank him for his lovely gift, she turned to the task of entertaining her other guests until dinner was announced. But as soon as the Corbys' butler concluded his invitation to the company at large, Sophie felt a touch upon her arm and, smiling, she turned to find Tony there.

"You have not forgotten your promise to take dinner with me, I hope, Miss Corby," he said.

"Not at all, sir," she replied. She glanced over in the direction where she had just seen him and found that her father and Mr. Rollo were eagerly conversing in loud tones, oblivious to the movement toward the dining room.

"I see that you have left a rather interesting discussion," she said, nodding her head in their direction. "I hope you were not forced to abandon it on my account." She smiled accusingly at him.

But Tony appeared quite unconcerned. "Oh, no. Indeed not. Sir John and Mr. Rollo are having a rather technical discussion about how to keep their hunters fit in the off-season. It is too complex for me—I really could not follow it." He smiled down at her so broadly that she could see how pleased he was to have her to himself.

Sophie felt a quickening response inside her breast, but she was not ready to thank him for his gift, and she had no intention of letting him off so easily.

"I wonder how the discussion began," she said, having a fairly good idea of the answer.

"Now let me see," said Tony with a frown of concentration. "I believe that I may have mentioned something inadvertently which might have opened the subject. Something about something a friend of mine once said. But I was only trying to make conversation, you know. I really care very little about it."

"Yes," said Sophie, "so you have told me." Her look left no doubt about her opinion of his motives.

And, indeed, she saw out the corner of her eye that her mother had just recalled her father to dinner, and that he was looking about the room for Sophie, his hand clasping Mr. Rollo's arm. When he spotted her entering the dining room with Tony, he frowned deeply and his face reddened quickly. Avoiding his eye, Sophie made for the safety of the table, knowing it was too late for Sir John to do anything about her dinner partner now.

In spite of the glares she sensed coming her way from time to time during the meal that followed, Sophie thought she had never enjoyed a birthday celebration more than she did that evening. Tony's companionship was at all times uplifting to her spirits. She felt strangely alive and unaccustomedly alert whenever she was with him. And this was the first time that she had sat so long beside him and had him so much to herself. By a fortunate coincidence, the couple to either side of them were also happy with their choices of dinner partners and very little in the way of interruptions came between them. Tony kept her amused with the half-serious, half-teasing sort of talk he seemed to make. And presently, she did find the right moment to thank him for his gift, in a trembling voice that did not conceal her delight.

"I am glad you liked it," he said, obviously pleased. "I have found myself rereading them of late and hoped you would not be offended to receive them from me." He watched for her reaction to his words, but Sophie lowered her eyelashes in confusion, unable to meet his direct gaze. Uncertain whether she should read too much into his meaning, she answered in a rallying tone.

"Of course not. How could I be? But I confess myself disappointed not to hear the birthday ode you wrote for me." She half-expected him to deny the existence of one, but to her surprise he did not.

"In that case, I shall tell it to you one day, but you must excuse me from reading it before anyone else. After Mr. Rollo's performance, I should be unmanned by the public attention."

Sophie looked up in surprise. "You mean there really is one? When shall I hear it? You really do mean to tell it to me?"

Tony's lips twitched in amusement, but he nodded sincerely. "I do. But I shall wait for the time to be right."

"And when shall that be?"

"Soon," he answered. "You'll remember that my friends do not consider me much of a poet, but I shall hope beyond hope that my poem does please you."

Sophie gave him a sceptical look, her head a bit to one side. "How do I know whether or not to believe you, Sir Tony? When I first met you, I thought you the most open of gentlemen. And yet, I have learned there are times when you are not always so guileless as you appear." She examined him from beneath her lashes, but Tony only grinned.

"Peculiar, isn't it, Miss Corby?" he agreed. Then turning his blue gaze on her he added, "I wonder, have you any theories as to the possible reason for my strange behaviour of late?" Sophie looked up to see his eyes twinkling merrily. His smile was so radiant it left her with no doubt as to his meaning. Her heart beat strangely within her, and she made no attempt to hide her answering dimples.

When dinner was nearly over, Tony remembered to tell her that she and her mother would soon be receiving a card from some of his friends to attend a salon and that he would be pleased to take them in his carriage if they would accept. Sophie told him she was certain they would be delighted to go and would send him a message as soon as they received their invitation.

"Good," said Tony. "I hope you will enjoy it. The salons are usually held in the afternoon, and they are remarkably informal. I think you will like the people you meet there. They are *not* all sportsmen," he finished with a chuckle.

Sophie laughed, but mostly at herself. During the past month in London she had come to realize that it was her own family and not Sir Tony who was eccentric.

The meal was too soon over and with it Tony's time alone with Sophie. For as soon as the gentlemen joined the ladies after their port, Sir John made certain that Mr. Rollo got the post nearest his daughter, and it was not until they parted for the evening that Sophie was able to speak to Tony again. As he took his leave of the entire family, he made a point of thanking Sophie's mother for the excellent dinner and finished by issuing an invitation.

"Lady Corby," he said. "My mother has requested me to invite you and Miss Corby to tea at her house next Thursday. She lives in Notting Hill, and I should be happy to escort you."

Lady Corby was almost flustered by the invitation, but after glancing once at Sophie's pleased expression, she accepted it with pleasure.

She was fully conscious that an invitation of this kind could mean that Sir Tony was anxious for his mother to meet and approve Sophie. But if she had not been, Sir John's frown would have alerted her. A time was agreed upon, and Tony took his leave, not forgetting to wish Sophie a happy birthday once again.

Sir John managed to hold his tongue until the last of the guests had departed, but since that last guest was Mr. Rollo, he was careful to say nothing until the door had closed behind him. Then, however, he immediately called Sophie to account, over the protests of his wife, for "sequestering herself with that Farnham fellow."

Ignoring Lady Corby's defense of her daughter he said, "How she could eat with a thistle-whipper like Farnham when Rollo had just delivered a birthday ode to her, I cannot imagine. Have you no sense of what is due to the young man, Sophie?"

"Certainly, Papa," lied Sophie, not wishing to raise her father's ire, "but Sir Tony had asked to be my dinner partner quite early in the evening before anyone else had. And I had no reason to refuse him. Why, Mr. Rollo never once raised the notion."

"Humpph!" snorted Sir John, only ruffled by this reasonable answer. "And Farnham saw to it that Rollo did not have the chance. Kept him busy talking to himself the whole evening. Well, I'll give him one thing. He's no slow top." Sophie repressed a smile, but her father's next remark was less to her liking.

"I do not like this scheme of his to take you to meet his mother. It smacks of something. I'll not say what, but I don't want you to encourage him, Sophie. He's not the man for you."

Lady Corby spoke quickly, "Oh, Sir John! I do not think you need fear that Sir Tony's invitation has any special significance. Why, there has been no hint of it. I should think he has just persuaded his mother to give us a treat in view of our limited acquaintance in Town. He has tried to make our time here as pleasant as possible. It is really most kind."

Her words seemed to have a beneficial effect upon her husband's temper, for he did not snort again, but mumbled something about not needing any kindness from *him*. Then he said, "Well, if that is the way it is, you may go, but I do not want you to make a habit of always being seen in his company. People might get the wrong impression. And there is no need for more acquaintances. We shall be gone from London soon, and we shall have no need for them then."

Sophie knew that what he was saying was all too true. She could not count on her father's staying in London even until the end of the social season. He would have scores of things to do to prepare for next November's hunting. But she was grateful to her mother for playing down the importance of Tony's invitation if it meant that her father would allow them to go. He seemed to have developed a strong objection to Tony since meeting Mr. Rollo, and she was in no doubt as to his mind. He wanted to have her married to Rollo before this year's hunting season could start.

Lady Corby was watching her daughter's face as she digested these thoughts. She had only recently begun to suspect that Sophie had a preference for Sir Tony and until tonight had not realized that it might be mutual. Up until now, Sir Tony had not singled Sophie out for his attention. He had always been careful not to embarrass her with too much obvious devotion and had instead acted the pleasant guest with them all. Now, it seemed otherwise, and while Lady Corby liked him very much, she was afraid that Sir John would not allow the suit to prosper, preferring as he clearly did the prospect of having Mr. Rollo for a son-in-law. She, however, planned to do her utmost to allow Sophie to have her choice.

CHAPTER EIGHT

THE DAY OF THE EXPEDITION to Notting Hill arrived, and both Lady Corby and Sophie could be glad that Sir John was not at home to see them off. He had left for his club earlier in the day and seemed to have forgotten their plans entirely. They hoped to be home before he could find them gone and recall his grievances on the occasion.

It was a brisk late-April day, unusually sunny but without too much wind, and Sophie considered it a grand day for a drive. Tony drove his team at a careful pace to Oxford Street and then faster as they passed the entrance to Hyde Park and headed out into the country. Sophie was seated beside her mother in the carriage so there was not much opportunity for her to converse with Tony in the city, but once they were beyond the rows of buildings, he was able to turn his head to give an occasional answer over his shoulder.

"Does your mother stay in the city for much of the year, Sir Tony?" enquired Lady Corby.

"Well, yes and no, Lady Corby," answered Tony. "You see, the house to which we are going is now mother's country place, but it is close enough to the city to allow her to drive in whenever she wishes. She keeps a town house open at all times and prefers never to be too far from it. But she has taken the house in Notting Hill so that she can pursue her more rural interests."

"Does she not visit you in Hampshire?" asked Sophie.

They could hear the amusement in Tony's voice as he answered, "No, never. She abhors the place. It reminds her too forcibly of my father. I cannot say that I blame her, but I, of course, was at school most of the time, so it is easier for me to forget that he was ever there. He seldom was in the holidays, anyway. He was away at the races."

"Theirs was not a happy marriage, then?" asked Lady Corby sympathetically.

"No," said Tony. Then after a pause he added impishly, "Miss Corby, I had hoped you would say voluntarily and rather spontaneously that at least it had produced me!" Sophie giggled by way of response and obliged him, although without the spontaneity for which he had wished. And even Lady Corby laughed at his impudence.

They arrived at Lady Farnham's before long. Indeed, Sophie was surprised at the quickness of the journey and could only credit the skill of Tony's driving, which had taken them over the roads at a spanking pace without causing them any discomfort. They found themselves at a charming Georgian house, which was somewhat larger than might be expected for a widow without her own fortune. Tony explained that his mother often entertained guests for days at a time, but that the house was now empty of company.

The door was opened by a respectable servant, who showed them into a bright, cheerful parlour and told them that her ladyship would be advised of their arrival. A fire was already burning in the grate, and early flowers had been arranged and distributed throughout the room. When Lady Corby admired them for their colour and variety, Tony explained that his mother was a skillful gardener and cultivated a wide assortment of bulbs.

They had sat conversing for no more than a few minutes, when the door to the garden burst open and a ghostly apparition with trailing white limbs entered. Lady Corby so far forgot herself as to issue a startled "oh," before covering her mouth in apology, for the spectre, on seeing them, let out with an enthusiastic cry of welcome. "Tony! My dearest! And dear, dear Sophia, I'll warrant! And this must be Lady Corby. Welcome, my dears, welcome." And with that, the startling creature, draped in layers of white gauze and lace, approached them with arms outstretched.

Tony went forward unperturbed to meet the apparition, who Sophie had guessed by now must be Lady Farnham, but he was frustrated in his attempt to plant a kiss on her cheek by all the layers of lace. Laughing at her own forgetfulness, Lady Farnham explained, "I don't wonder that I scared you out of your wits, but you see I was only coming to see whether you had arrived and as soon as I saw you, I forgot how I was dressed. I daresay Bacon is trying to find me to tell me you are here."

Tony was smiling down affectionately at the diminutive ghost beside him, but Sophie and her mother still could not make out any features behind the as yet unexplained mask. Now Tony presented them, and they shook hands with her ladyship, who was fully gloved, as well.

"I imagine you may be wondering what has possessed me to dress like a haunt at this time of the day and are too well-bred to ask—although saying 'at this time of the day' is rather ridiculous, I suppose," bubbled Lady Farnham. "Well, I was simply outdoors tending my bees and I had forgotten exactly what time to expect you, even though Tony is always punctual. Or so he tells me. I do not pay that much attention to the hour, myself. But anyway, as I am already done up this way, I will not change just yet if Sophie would like to come outside with me to see the bees."

Sophie, her eyes wide with delight, was finding herself more enchanted by the moment with Lady Farnham's artless chatter, and she had already determined from which parent Sir Tony had got his open manner. Glancing once his way and seeing his satisfied expression, she accepted eagerly, but was surprised soon after to hear her own mother's voice asking wistfully, "Might I come, too?" Turning, she saw that Lady Corby had fallen under the spell of this strange warm creature as certainly as she had done herself.

"My dear Lady Corby, of course!" exclaimed Lady Farnham happily. "I did not mean to exclude you at all. You must understand that I am so used to being refused by so many of my friends that I have assumed only the young people will have the heart for it. But you are so pretty and young yourself, I daresay you fear nothing at all."

Lady Corby accepted this strange reading of her character with no more than a flicker of the eyelids. She was surprised to find herself growing braver just upon hearing Lady Farnham's assumption. And, in no more than a moment, they had followed their hostess out the door and around the side of the house to a sunny flower garden. Here and there they could see individual bees hovering and closing in on a bright flower. But before they could discover the location of the beehive, Lady Farnham remembered something.

"We must be very careful," she told them quietly. "You see, I have just robbed them of their honey and they are not terribly pleased with me at the moment. But you must protect yourselves and if we do not threaten them again, I am certain they will forget all about it and let us watch them closely. Here," she said, beginning to unravel a swath of gauze from around her head, "you must drape this over your head and shoulders loosely, not just your face, for they can just as well sting the top of your head or your ear. So I have learned to my discomfort.'' Sophie offered the first piece of material to her mother, who obediently placed it over her head and shoulders with Tony's help. And Lady Corby continued to unwrap pieces from about her own head until they began to make out the outline of her face beneath.

"No, no dear," said the now visible lady in response to Sophie's protest that she did not want to strip her of her own protection. "I shall not need so much just to watch them, you see. I only wrapped myself so completely because I knew I was going to anger them. But we shall all be perfectly safe with about two pieces of lace or gauze each. Just be certain not to leave any bare spots! Tony," she asked as an afterthought, "shall I have Bacon bring you some or do you not intend to join us.''

"No, thank you, Mother," he said, as though grateful for the reprieve. "I shall just sit over here and enjoy the prospect of three lovely spirits in my mother's garden." He watched them off and took a seat on the ground beneath a spreading elm.

"Just as you like, love," said Lady Farnham as they left him to cross the lawn. "But don't let him fool you, my dears," she said in an undervoice to her guests. "He would have you think he is too frightened of the bees, but he often helps me with them. That boy!" She tut-tutted affectionately.

Sophie smiled beneath her layers of gauze. She felt a bit ridiculous traipsing across the lawn this way in the wake of Tony's mother, but at the same time she marvelled to think that but a few minutes ago they had not even made her acquaintance. Lady Farnham had the same gift of putting one at one's ease as her son—or perhaps it was the other way around. At any rate, both Sophie and her mother felt remarkably at home, considering they were about to do something they had never done before.

"Is this what one *always* wears when tending bees, Lady Farnham?" asked Lady Corby. "It is odd that I have never noticed anyone dressed this way in the country, when I think of the quantity of honey we consume."

Her hostess laughed delightedly. "Heavens, my dear! I do not have the faintest idea what anyone else wears to tend bees, but it *is* what I wear. And it works rather well, as you will see. One can see through the gauze or the lace, but the bees cannot penetrate them to sting. Now, here we are," she said as they reached an aged tree trunk with a gaping hole in its side.

As Sophie and her mother could see and hear, they had now arrived at the hive, where an alarming number of bees were buzzing about the entrance. They slowed their pace instinctively and crept cautiously closer. Lady Farnham gestured to them to stop a few steps away and lowered her voice again before speaking.

"I'm afraid they are still rather upset about the theft of their honey, but I did think we should have some with our tea this afternoon. If we wait here, perhaps they will settle down a bit."

Sophie peered rather anxiously at the bees, hoping that their anger would not extend to her and her mother, who were, after all, innocent of any wrongdoing. But after watching them for a while, she decided that their buzzings and hoverings were random and without harmful intent, and she began to relax and become curious. It occurred to her that for all the honey she had eaten, she had never much thought of the bees that produced it, and she began to wonder how they did it. She ventured a question in a cautious whisper.

"Lady Farnham, how do the bees make honey?"

"I really do not know, my dear," answered that lady imperturbably. "But I can tell you what I do know. All of the bees that you see out here are called the workers. It is they who collect the nectar from the flowers with which to make the honey. And they keep the hive clean, take care of the baby bees and feed the queen. The queen does nothing more than have babies, but without her, the hive should die. There are no drones here now for you to see because it is not the swarming season yet."

"What are the drones?"

"You may well ask, my dear," said her ladyship with surprising emphasis. "They are the suitors of the queen bee. The one that is chosen to mate with the queen does so only once, and then she is able to produce baby bees indefinitely and keep the nest supplied with workers, as you well can see. She really is a remarkable creature.''

''Then what happens to the drones, the ones that do not succeed and the one who does?''

Lady Farnham replied firmly, ''They are killed. And it is no wonder, really, for they are rather despicable creatures. They do not turn a hand in the hive, and they rob the babies of food. So the workers kill them. It is always a surprise to me that the queen chooses a drone for a husband. If it were me, I should prefer a worker. They are much more fascinating.''

''They certainly are,'' agreed Sophie, wide-eyed. She watched the bees' comings and goings with more attention now, but presently Lady Farnham spoke again.

''I really cannot like the drones,'' she sighed. ''They do so remind me of Sir Geoffrey.''

''Sir Geoffrey?'' enquired both her visitors.

''Tony's father,'' she explained in a tone of great confidentiality. ''You will think me horrid to say so, I know, but he really wasn't so very different from a drone. My mother always did say that honesty was my worst fault. And I am only being truthful when I say it. Sir Geoffrey really did nothing for me but help me to produce Tony, and beyond that he served his own pleasure, and yes, robbed his own child, too. It was a miracle that anything of the estate survived him, but

Tony has worked wonders in restoring it. He is such a dear boy.''

Sophie was fascinated by these disclosures and could only guess at the shock on her mother's countenance underneath all her draperies. But, in truth, Lady Corby was listening with more sympathy than censure.

"It's no wonder you find them so interesting, Lady Farnham," was all she said.

"Aren't they?" agreed Tony's mother, happy to have her enthusiasm shared. "You can have no idea how hard the workers do work. They live for only a short time during the summer months because they work so hard. And it is a great mystery how they are able to find the sources for their honey. But if I were a bee, I should much rather be a worker than a drone, or even the queen—her life is really quite boring—for in spite of their short lives they taste all the richest things in life. They sample all the flowers and still manage to care for the young. I do so admire the workers."

They watched for a while longer, and Lady Farnham explained more of the bees' activities until something in their behaviour set her to thinking. She lowered her voice again and spoke in a pensive tone. "If you will excuse me ladies, I am beginning to think that it would be wiser for us to retire. I do not like the look of that group swarming over there. If it were summer, I should say that they were about to search for a new hive, but since it is not, I think they may have recognized me and decided that I have brought two more accomplices to rob them.''

Sophie and her mother retired hastily, with Lady Farnham courageously protecting their rear until they were safely away from the hive. ''Tony would never forgive me if I invited you here for tea and then subjected you to bee stings,'' she said, laughing. ''But I am so glad you came with me to see them. You will enjoy your teacakes and honey all the more for seeing where it is come from. And the dear bees, though they are frightfully clever, will have forgotten me by the time I go back for more,'' she added gaily.

They rejoined Tony, who had been watching them lazily from a semi-reclining position under the tree. Sophie watched him rise effortlessly as they approached and noted with pleasure that his coat looked as fresh as if he had not just been lying on the open ground. He seemed as at home in the country as he was on the dance floor at Almack's, and she found it an attractive quality, and one of which he seemed totally unaware.

''Have the 'dear bees' chased you off?'' he asked, his eyes twinkling at the sight of the three apparitions.

''Of course not, silly boy,'' his mother said untruthfully. ''It *is* time for our tea, though, so perhaps you would help Sophia off with her drapes, and I shall help her mother.''

Strangely absorbed in watching Tony rise to meet them, Sophie had forgotten the ridiculous picture the three of them must make, but now she hastily set to work to remove her layers of gauze and found them caught on the small buttons of her gown in back. With a grin, Tony came to her assistance.

"Hold still," he commanded her cheerfully and then added in an eerie voice, " 'and I shall extract you from my mother's web,' said the spider to the fly." But instead of working from one end of the material, he began near her head, slowly lifting the drapes from around her face and rearranging them toward the back. She felt the gentleness of his hands as they freed her eyes, nose, cheeks and ears, and a curious thrill shot through her. And knowing these sensations to be most improper, still she dared not move, so rapt was she by the tenderness in his movements. When Tony was done liberating her face, he stepped back and looked at her approvingly.

"Ah," he said with slow satisfaction. "That is much better." Sophie was aware that the layers of material had now taken the appearance of billowing clouds framing her face. She felt herself blush from her cheeks down to the tips of her toes, but was so spellbound she could do nothing to avoid his admiring gaze. He stood there a moment more, smiling down at Sophie, seemingly unhampered by her mother's presence, until Lady Farnham came to her rescue.

"Let me see what you have done, Tony," she said, coming around to face Sophie. Looking her over critically, she nodded her head in agreement. "Yes, she looks absolutely divine. But you must not tease her, you naughty boy. Turn around, dear," she said to Sophie, "and let me free your buttons. You must not mind Tony. He has a good eye for beauty, but I will not let him do you up like a posy."

Sophie laughed as the spell was broken. She was grateful that Tony's mother had not been offended by the scene that had just taken place before her. On the contrary, Lady Farnham seemed quite happy with her two guests, and Sophie suspected that she had come to her assistance with the generous intention of sparing her blushes. Now that Lady Farnham's own drapes were removed, Sophie could get a look at Tony's mother for the first time. She had the same almost green-blue eyes as Tony's, with something about the shape of the nose and cheekbones that was similar, too. But her hair was turned grey and was, after being so long under covers, a bit askew. And in her face there was a strange sense, it occurred to Sophie, of a child who had aged too quickly and been magically restored to youth.

Lady Farnham herded them into the house, and before long they were having tea in a charming room which looked out over the flower garden. It was too early in the year for the perennials to be in bloom, but the beds were bursting with the brighter colors of daffodils, tulips and hyacinths. Lady Corby complimented Tony's mother upon the view.

"Oh, do you like it?" said Tony's mother, clasping her hands together happily. "I designed it myself. I always wanted a room where I could sit and feel that I was really outdoors. And later in the year, when it is not so chilly, I can open these doors and let the breeze with the scent of the flowers sweep right in. It is heavenly."

As she spoke, Sophie could almost feel the cool summer breeze scented with roses. She closed her eyes for a second to imagine it and, when she opened them, realized that Tony's were upon her. He was grinning, obviously quite aware of what she had been experiencing, and she had to restrain herself from laughing upon being found out.

"You must be careful, Mama," he said wickedly. "Or you will put our guests to sleep. No, do not blush," he said as Lady Corby started as if from a trance and Sophie began to protest. "You must understand that my mother has worked this spell before, and it is not at all uncommon for one to fall asleep in this room."

Lady Farnham laughed. "Impudent boy," she said. "But indeed, he is right, with the only exception being that I have nothing to do with it. It is the room. I frequently take little unplanned naps in it myself. I do love it so." She looked at her son gratefully, and Sophie suddenly realized that Tony must have provided this house for her. If, as they had both said, the Farnham estates had been in serious straits when Sir Geoffrey died, it stood to reason that Tony must have had to provide for his mother.

The tea soon revived them all, and Lady Corby begged to be shown the rest of the house. Lady Farnham was quite happy to oblige, and a tour commenced. But it did not pass as rapidly as they had expected, for every room held further evidence of Lady Farnham's enthusiasms, from butterfly collections to the manufacture of miniature furniture. Indeed, one whole room was filled with beautiful doll's houses, completely carpeted, curtained and furnished.

"Oh, they're lovely," cried Sophie. "What do you do with them?"

"I give them to friends' grandchildren," said Lady Farnham airily, "having none of my own, of course. Tony has promised me to have scores someday, so I have saved my best examples for them." She threw him a look of playful reproof before continuing. "You see, I love to decorate houses, but it would be much too expensive to keep decorating my own, so I use bits of scraps to make these toy ones."

"What is this?" asked Lady Corby, pointing to something in one of the doll's houses. She was as fascinated by the houses as Sophie was.

"Oh, that?" said Lady Farnham proudly. "That is a model of Count Rumford's stove. I often heard him speak at the Royal Institute and always fancied a little stove for one of my houses. Perhaps you would care to go with me to one of the lectures. Sir Humphrey Davy speaks there occasionally and, my dear, I cannot tell you what fun it is to watch one of his little experiments!''

They chatted on until Sophie's mother realized that they must be heading back to Town. Their reluctance to leave was matched by Lady Farnham's dismay to see them go.

''Oh, I shall hate to lose you,'' she said. ''I ought to have thought of it earlier and perhaps you could have come with me.''

''To where, Mama?'' said Tony.

''Why to be magnetized, dearest,'' she said, seriously sorry for her omission.

To both Sophie's and Lady Corby's surprise, Tony hooted with laughter. ''Magnetized? What, again, Mother? I thought you had done with magnetizing when the effect of those metallic tractors was found to have been produced by the imagination.''

Lady Farnham did not seem in the least offended. She answered blithely. ''Oh, Tony. Did you think I would be such a silly goose as to fall for that trick again? Shame on you. That was so long ago. No, this magnetism is more in the nature of an animal magnetism, not the mineral sort. It is quite new. A friend of mine in Town has invited a doctor from France to come show it to us. And you need not worry that I shall waste a penny on it.''

"How is it supposed to work?" asked her son in pure amusement.

"Why, I don't know precisely," she admitted. "Something to do with fluids emanating from the body which can be sent forth in currents at the will of the magnetizer. It is supposed to induce a state of somnambulism, and one is supposed to release oneself to a belief in its curative powers. He promises it can cure rheumatism and gout and—oh, I forget—all sorts of things."

Tony's eyebrows rose in playful scepticism, and Lady Farnham tapped his chest reprovingly before presenting her cheek to be kissed. "Oh, go on, silly boy. I know it's all a hoax. But just think what fun," she said to Lady Corby and Sophie as they parted, "to be stared at by a French doctor who's doing his best to put one into a trance!" Sophie laughed and Lady Corby was surprised to find that she was heartily wishing she could go to be magnetized, too.

Later, after setting them down again in Berkeley Square, Tony sat awhile in his carriage, thinking. He reflected happily that he had spent the whole of the afternoon in Sophie's company without seeing her yawn once, and he was quite certain that her thoughts had not drifted during the visit. The awakening he had wished for seemed to have come to pass, and he only hoped that her alertness had something to do with himself.

Sophia, Tony thought. She is wise. And clever and funny, as well. He suspected she had a mind that was as eager to enjoy life as his own was, and he wondered how she would like to enjoy it with him.

CHAPTER NINE

THE HAPPINESS THAT SOPHIE and her mother had experienced during their visit to Lady Farnham's stayed with them for days and even managed to survive Sir John's bad temper on the subject. But another, grander treat was in store for them.

As Tony had promised, Sophie soon received a note inviting her and Lady Corby to an afternoon salon, but to their great surprise, the paper bore the heading of Holland House. Sophie had not thought to wonder from whom among Tony's many friends the invitation would come, but she was thrown into a fluster by the thought of attending one of the most celebrated salons of the day. The message was written in a friendly style, but the final words caused Sophie's heart to sink within her, for they commanded her in no uncertain terms to bring some of her poetry with her.

"Do you think we should accept?" Sophie asked her mother fearfully as they read the note together in the parlour. It was morning, and Sir John had gone to his club early and missed the post.

Lady Farnham looked strangely pensive and replied in an absent tone of voice, "Oh, I think so, yes. One would not like to refuse such a gracious invitation. Holland House!" she exclaimed almost in a whisper. "I never expected this." Sophie had little cause to wonder at her mother's reaction, for, except for her father's hunting companions, they had never moved in such an elevated circle. It was not Lord Holland's title which was intimidating, for both Sir John and Lady Corby were well-connected and counted a number of peers among their cousins and in-laws. It was the extraordinary position held by the Hollands in society. If all one said about it was true, Holland House was habitually visited by the greatest minds in all England, even Europe.

A note from Tony informed them of his intention to take them in his carriage, and Sophie bravely searched through her poems to select the best specimens among them. She tried to look at them objectively without regard to their subject, as she supposed an accomplished poet might do, but she hoped that Lady Holland's command had been written merely out of politeness and that she would not remember to ask to hear them.

The morning of their proposed outing, the Corbys sat down to breakfast together before Sir John left for his club. He was in a cheerful mood that day, having just the night before run into an old comrade from the Pytchley hunt. The two had spent the evening reliving past runs, and Sir John had been particularly amused by a real "tickler" which his friend, fresh from the field, had experienced this season. He had been repeating it in full detail for the benefit of his wife and daughter during the meal.

"So Bumley was leading the field just then," he related, "having got a nick by a turn, when what should Puggy do but lead the hounds into a sheep pen. There was no passing through it, for the gate was shut fast and there was not enough room to jump into it or out of it. The dogs were confused by the sheep's scent, of course, and kept milling around the pen where the whipper-in could not get to them, until the huntsman, by a wild chance, spotted old Pug breaking cover again and tally-hoed the hounds. As soon as they left the pen at his urging, they hit off the scent, and Bumley was on their tails. But his horse hit a toe on an anthill and plunged him into a hedge so deeply that it took two men to extract him!" Sir John chuckled gleefully at his friend's discomfort, and Lady Corby smiled at his obvious pleasure.

Sophie's smile was rather absent for her nervousness had increased overnight. It was not the trip to Holland House which had her in a flutter, but the thought that she might be called on to show Lady Holland her poetry. And she had been wondering how best to punish Tony for divulging her secret pastime to such an important critic.

"A charming story, dear," her mother was saying. "You must give my regards to Lord Bumley and ask him to dine with us soon. Shall you be seeing him today?"

"Yes, by Gad! Look at the hour!" exclaimed Sir John. "I promised to meet him at Tattersall's. He's interested in a bay gelding there, just above sixteen hands, which he hopes will carry him, and he wants my opinion. He rides fourteen stone, you know. Must take every chance he gets to find one that can support him."

"By all means, John, you must hurry," said Lady Corby with sincere encouragement. "He must not lose such an opportunity."

Sir John wiped the last crumbs from his lips and rose from the table. "And, how shall you two occupy yourselves today?" he asked indifferently.

Sophie, her mind already fixed on the subject, was about to blurt out their plans for the day when her mother cut in abruptly. "We are going to call on some friends this afternoon, and I plan to put a new trim on one of Sophie's dresses this morning," she said calmly, ignoring her daughter's stare. Sophie was wondering why her mother should already be speaking of the Hollands as friends and how she could mention the proposed outing in the same breath as her needlework. But Sir John was halfway out the door before his question was answered, and there was no point in pursuing it.

"Enjoy yourselves," he called as the door closed behind him. The slight interest he had shown in their activities did not offend the two ladies, for the fact that he had shown any at all was a fair barometer of his own degree of happiness at the moment.

Lady Corby, with a strangely scrupulous honesty, did occupy her morning as she had said she would, and with Sophie's help the dress was trimmed by noon. Tony arrived, and the three set out as before, but this time in the direction of Kensington. The weather was again propitious, which had the result of making Sophie think that her fears had been for nothing. And before she could entertain them again, they had left the turnpike road and were on a curving drive which cut through Lord Holland's trees. At the gate house, Tony did nothing more than wave to a guard with a familiar gesture before negotiating the remaining yards of the circular drive to the house.

One view of Holland House and Sophie could understand the attraction it held for both the Fox family who occupied it and its visitors from all over the world. Its style was a mixture of both classic and Gothic, reality and fantasy. The south side, which they now approached, was in the shape of a perfectly symmetrical "U," but was at the same time adorned with a magnificent Gothic arcade the entire length of the ground floor and a balcony on the first floor. The main portal was located dead centre in an imposing bay structure, flanked with rows of Gothic windows and surmounted by a dome. Twin towers topped the northern corners of the central wing. All this Sophie saw quickly as they drove past, but the whole of the fabulous structure was more than her mind could absorb in one brief glance.

Once inside, they were taken upstairs and greeted by a stout, strong man with a large head and thick, round spectacles. His legs were thick and his accent Scotch, but Tony greeted him with sincere respect and introduced him to the ladies as Mr. Allen. The gentleman welcomed them with the air of a trusted member of the family, without pretension but with great goodwill, and conversed with them congenially for a moment. He carried about with him a sort of diary which he explained was one of Lady Holland's "Dinner Books" into which he would add their names as her ladyship's guests. Sophie was curious to see that Tony seemed to accept Mr. Allen as a manner of host, and she would have thought him Lord Holland's personal secretary if it had not been for the extreme respect Tony seemed to accord him.

Mr. Allen explained that the guests were gathering in the Sir Joshua Room, and he directed them through the Gilt Room where, surrounded by the magnificence of an ornate ceiling, marble busts on pillars and rectangular wall compartments with the fleur de lis argent of the original owner, a rather small table had been set for ten. With the certainty of habit, Tony led them to the next room where a much larger crowd was standing in various groups, each lively with conversation.

Lady Corby had taken Tony's arm and entered the room first, for Sophie had stopped for a moment to stare up at the ceiling of the Gilt Room and had lagged slightly behind. As she entered, she saw that the others had been approached by a distinguished-looking gentleman with a limp, and she quickened her step to join them. But she was stopped suddenly by an imperious voice calling out, "Have the goodness to close the door!"

Looking about her to discover its source and fearful that the command was intended for herself, Sophie spied an elegant woman seated at the end of the room. Her chair was elevated slightly, and her feet rested on a small stool, which somehow gave her the appearance of being upon a throne. She stared at Sophie and then beckoned to her, although mercifully she did not seem to expect Sophie to close the enormous doors. Darting one quick look back at Tony for support, Sophie found that he was still speaking to the gentleman, but he smiled encouragement, so she straightened her shoulders and moved forward. Rightfully assuming that the seated lady was Lady Holland, she curtsied and received a nod of welcome.

"You are Miss Corby, are you not?" asked her hostess. "I saw you enter with Sir Tony, and he did promise to bring you to us today. And that lady on his arm is your mother?"

Sophie affirmed it. Lady Holland paused for a moment and gazed at Sophie's mother, but her look was neither unkind nor unfriendly. She turned back to Sophie and, with an enigmatic expression, spoke one sentence as if in explanation of her curiosity. "Your father's name is not unknown to me."

Sophie was uncertain whether to respond with a polite "oh?" or just a smile, but before she could decide, Lady Holland had moved on to another topic.

"Tony tells us that you write poetry, my child. Is this true? He seems not to have heard any of it, but is remarkably confident of its being good."

Sophie's all but forgotten nervousness now returned full force, but Lady Holland's last words were more disconcerting than the recollection of her poetry. Sophie blushed and replied truthfully, "Yes, I do write some. But as to its being any good or not, Lady Holland, I cannot vouch. Sir Tony is extraordinarily kind and perhaps has let his sense of kindness mislead him."

She had hoped that these words would satisfy Lady Holland's obligation to enquire about her poems, but to her horror, they seemed to have no such effect. With no apparent awareness of Sophie's embarrassment, her hostess replied simply, "Well, let us see," and, clapping her hands together in a regal gesture, called for her guests' attention.

"Everyone please be silent now," she commanded. "Miss Corby is going to favour us with a poetry reading."

Sophie felt her knees fail beneath her as the heads in the enormous room turned to listen. It did not matter that not a face among them looked unfriendly. All she could think was that this room was often filled, perhaps three times a week, with the greatest names in all Europe, from Byron to Tallyrand, and she was now about to expose herself to them. She fumbled in her reticule for the papers she had brought, but her brain was seething with anger against Tony for getting her into this fix. And at the same time, she could think of no other who could save her. Her eyes darted about, searching for his face amongst the crowd, but found that he was the only person not watching her. He was speaking in a low voice to a small, dark man, whose bright eyes stared at her while he knitted his brows.

Hopeless now, she opened the pages in her hand and looked through them for the poem she thought her best. Her hands had begun to shake, and she feared that her voice would die inside her throat if she tried to speak. She cleared it once or twice and was about to begin in a tremulous squeak, when a voice spoke at her elbow.

"May I, your ladyship?" She looked up and found the gentleman to whom Tony had been speaking. She had assumed that he must be addressing Lady Holland, but his eyes were on her, and in spite of his mode of address, there was no mockery in them. Instead, smiling kindly, he held out his hand for the papers. Dumbly, she relinquished them, wondering weakly what he intended, but knowing that whatever he chose to do would be more merciful than allowing her to read it herself.

The gentleman looked the poem over briefly and then, with a smile of pleasure, began to read. His voice, though he did not strain to raise it, filled the room with clear, beautiful tones.

> "Wilt though begin my life, my love, My leaves unfurl with warmth above, My roots draw forth like arms below, Thy gentle heart my seed to sew."

The room was silent as he read on. Sophie stared at him, mesmerized by the sound of her own words on this stranger's lips. The words themselves, she knew, were not the greatest that this room had heard, and would not likely be heard in public again. It should have hurt to hear her most private thoughts revealed unsparingly, but the beauty of his voice carried them up and raised them to a level of universal feeling. The silence in the room confirmed that the others present, though not so nearly touched as Sophie by the words themselves, were experiencing the same hypnosis and the wrench on the emotions that she felt as he read her final couplet.

> "Until my wounded heart shall mend, I'll wait, love's fallow field to tend."

There was silence for a moment more, and then applause filled the room. Sophie found herself clapping along with them, although soon she realized that part of the applause was for her. The gentleman who had read her poem accepted the acclaim as though accustomed to it and turned to bow to her as the authoress. Unable to acknowledge it with the same degree of confidence that he had shown, she was grateful to be saved by the approach of some of the guests, who greeted her with enthusiasm and clapped her unknown saviour upon the back. At a word from Lady Holland, who was still seated beside her, Sophie turned to find that lady smiling.

"Delightful, my dear," she said, obviously pleased with the success of her guests. "And what a treat! He will not perform at my request, I assure you. I can only assume that he makes exceptions when the poet is sufficiently young and beautiful to gain his attention. But I do not mean to diminish your own accomplishments. It was a lovely poem, and you should be told that I am no poor critic. Wasn't it lovely, Henry?"

Sophie found that the distinguished-looking gentleman with a limp who had first greeted Tony and her mother had now joined them. It was Lord Holland.

"Yes, it was," he agreed kindly, presenting himself to her. "You must allow me to thank you for giving us such a treat. And, my wife is being quite truthful. I would be embarrassed to recount the number of times she has tried to persuade Mr. Kean to give us a read-

ing, but he will not oblige. She has had to stop for fear
he will no longer come to see us."

Sophie's jaw relaxed with astonishment and she
hoped her mouth had not fallen open. Edmund Kean
had read her poem! Edmund Kean, the great Shake-
spearian actor! She searched for him and meeting his
eye, smiled her gratitude. He bowed in return, and the
gesture betrayed no sense of grandeur. And now she
understood why he had called her "your ladyship," for
this man, for all his greatness, was not of the nobility.
He moved in aristocratic circles as a man of talent, but
as a social inferior, and titles of distinction would not
be a clear matter to him. A question leapt to her mind,
but just as quickly she found the answer.

Tony! It was Tony who had got him to read the poem
for her. And suddenly she realized that he was near. He
was by her side speaking to Lord Holland, who was
thanking him for bringing her to their gathering.

"Perhaps Miss Corby would care to be shown some
of the house, Tony," their host was saying. "It is a fine
day for a walk in the Southern Arcades, although I
must caution you about the balustrades. They are in
need of repair. You will forgive me for not taking you
round myself, Miss Corby, but this leg of mine is crip-
pled with gout. And Tony knows the way. He will not
lose you." Lord Holland smiled with genuine cordial-
ity, and Sophie found herself leaving the scene which
had caused her such anxiety on the safety of Tony's
arm.

They did not speak until they had passed again through the Gilt Room and were descending the Grand Staircase. Sophie realized that she was holding on to Tony with a closeness that was directly related to all that had passed before. Now, with the sound of voices far in the distance, she breathed a sigh and loosened her hold slightly.

"Lord Holland is most congenial," she said presently, all the while feeling the inadequacy of her words to describe the overwhelming kindness that a man in possession of such influence had shown to a person of no consequence like herself.

"There is not a man better liked in all England," said Tony gently, "nor will there ever be."

Sophie was happy to hear him express himself so seriously. For all the gaiety that surrounded him habitually, she had always sensed the more serious depth inside him. She ought, she realized, to call him to account for having placed her in such a horrid position, but the result had been so unexpectedly gratifying that she could not be angry. She had been shaken though, so for a moment, she had no wish to talk about what had happened and asked about the house instead.

Tony obliged her, seeming to understand her reluctance. They strolled about a few of the public rooms, talking about the paintings, tapestries and objets d'art until Tony suggested walking in the arcades.

"Who is Mr. Allen?" Sophie asked as they stepped outdoors. The lawn sloped down in front of them until it reached the hay fields below. A mild breeze blew over them from the south and softly stirred the curls at her temples.

"Allen?" said Tony, evidently pleased by her question. "Allen is, or perhaps I should say was, a doctor who was engaged to take care of the Hollands' first son. Their children have not been strong. But his true calling is as an historical scholar, and he now tends the library. He's a man of enormous talent. Lady Holland orders him about like a dog, but they are both sincerely attached to him and would find it difficult to get along without him."

"She is rather imperious, is she not?" asked Sophie.

Tony chuckled. "Yes," he stated baldly. "But the Hollands' friends keep coming. There is no other place which so warmly encourages talent in all its forms. And perhaps they all understand. She is not received at court, you see, because of her divorce, so this is her own little court. And rather more congenial than the other, I should say."

"I see," said Sophie pensively. She paused for a moment and then added, "I *should* be very angry with you, Sir Tony, for exposing me so dreadfully."

"But you are not?" he asked with a smile.

She smiled and shook her head. "No. But only because you sent Mr. Kean to save me. How did you persuade him to do it?"

"He's my friend," said Tony, shrugging. "He needed no persuasion."

Sophie regarded him quizzically. "Yet he will not perform for Lady Holland, and she might be thought to be a friend."

Tony shook his head. "Not really. Kean is careful to distinguish between friends and patrons. He gives of his art freely to his friends, but he will not perform for his patrons, no matter how much they implore him. His talent is all he has, you see, and if he allowed that to be ordered about like a common street show he should be left with nothing."

"Then how did *you* come to be his friend?"

Tony's mouth curled upwards at the recollection of a memory. "Remember that I told you I sometimes enjoyed the pleasures of Town late at night?" She nodded. "Well, while I was at Eton, I was taken by one of the masters to a dinner at Hummums Hotel in Covent Garden to meet Kean. It was there that I became aware of his great tolerance for drink *and* his ability to perform beautifully when he is three sheets to the wind."

She giggled. "Well, I cannot tell you how grateful I was to see him, although if I had known who he was I would likely have swooned."

They had walked out onto the porch now, and Tony stopped to sit upon the low stone railings. He smiled at her, and she smiled back, her dimples appearing suddenly beneath the ribbons to her bonnet. As they looked at each other, Tony's smile faded gently, and he began to gaze earnestly in a manner which Sophie found most disconcerting. She dropped her eyelids before his searching look, but could do nothing to hide her dimples.

"I liked your poem, Sophie," he said softly. She felt a thrill as he spoke her first name. It had never sounded so much like a caress. "Is that how you feel about love?"

She was conscious in her confusion of his eyes upon her, but she did not turn away. "Yes," she said, not daring to look up.

"And yet you do not wish to be married?"

Sophie did not know how to answer. She realized suddenly that she did very much wish to be married, that the yearnings she had to love and be loved could thus be fulfilled. But only if her husband could also be her lover. Remembering the talk they had had on their first carriage ride together, she knew that her feelings for Tony had undergone a rapid development, but she could not overcome her present shyness to contradict the things she had told him that day. She kept her head lowered and did not answer, hoping he would understand that her silence was a denial of those earlier feelings.

When she did not answer, Tony spoke again in a lighter tone. "I still have not recited for you the poem I wrote for your birthday."

Sophie's head came up with eagerness. "Did you really write one?"

"Of course, didn't I say so?"

She dimpled again. "Yes, you did. But I assumed that you would conveniently forget about it."

Tony grinned at this accusation, but there was a challenge in his expression. "Then I see that I shall have to prove my veracity. Would you care to hear it now?"

"Yes," Sophie said, placing herself beside him on the railing and folding her hands as though ready to be entertained. "I await your pleasure." She felt extraordinarily light-hearted and had more or less forgotten where they were.

"All right," said Tony, an assessing glint in his eye. "Here goes." He placed his hand upon his heart, and Sophie giggled again before he started. With no paper in hand to remind him of the words, he began. His voice was slightly teasing.

"Though I ought to write a sonnet
On your face, your eyes, your bonnet,
Citing queens or goddesses recalled to mind from ancient lore,
Still my muse can't be relied on,
Simple words I'm now tongue-tied on,
Fearing to be thought a silly fool, a pest or crushing bore.

"For no words describe your beauty.
Birthday odes seem but a duty
When they try to take the place of gazing with adoring eyes.

Odes may laudify your meekness,
Ignorant of your uniqueness,
Sounding with a ring of falseness, something that
I do despise."

Sophie's eyes had twinkled throughout his recital, but as the words of this verse sank in, she lowered her lashes and started to blush. And now, as he began the last verse, Tony's voice slowed. He took her hand in his and turned it palm upwards, stroking it gently. She could feel strange waves of heat running through her as she listened to his final words.

"So though I ought to speak of Hestia,
Artemis and Hypermnestra,
Any thought of these beside you strikes me as a bit
amiss.
My thoughts turn to Aphrodite
That through her you will invite me
To receive my heart's desire, a tender, precious
birthday kiss."

Sophie's head jerked up as she realized what he had said. A startled "oh" escaped her lips, and she was reminded suddenly of her flight up the inn stairs so many days ago. She had almost fallen under the spell of Tony's soft words, but now as she looked at him, she saw that his lips were twitching and he was trying not to laugh. She half-suspected that his request was in earnest, but he could not help being amused by the shock on her face.

"A birthday—" Sophie did not finish the phrase. "And what, pray, is that, Sir Tony?"

His expression was at once innocent of any artifice. "A birthday kiss," he repeated in a reasonable tone. "It is a tradition in my family. Is it not in yours?" A glint of humour danced about his eyes.

"No," said Sophie, blushing again as he repeated the word *kiss*. "It is not," she said, striving to sound firmer than her inclination would have her be.

"Too bad," said Tony, not daunted in the least. "In that case, do you care to oblige me?"

Sophie tried to glare at him ominously, but his impudence had robbed her of all control of her dimples. Nevertheless, she reminded him in a severe tone, "Sir Tony, I am not a member of your family."

Tony responded with a mysterious sparkle that set her heart to fluttering. "No, you're not," he said softly, bending slowly towards her. "Not yet."

Sophie waited, as though mesmerized, to meet his lips as they came towards hers. She closed her eyes dreamily and felt the warmth of Tony's face as he stooped ever closer. But suddenly he jerked away as a voice came clearly from the doorway.

"Ah, here you are." Sophie opened her eyes to see her mother emerging from the front door on the arm of Lord Holland. She felt as though she had been roughly awakened from a beautiful dream, and she looked about her wonderingly, surprised to find that she was still at Holland House. For the past many minutes, she had not been aware of her surroundings, only of Tony's eyes upon her. She looked for him and saw that he had covered his own confusion admirably by stepping forward to meet Lady Corby and their host.

"I fear that Sophia and I must be returning to Town, Sir Tony. Sir John will wonder what has become of us."

"Are you not staying to dinner?" asked Lord Holland, seemingly with sincere disappointment.

"No," said Tony. Then he added with an impudent grin, "We were not invited."

Both Sophie and her mother turned to their host with shocked expressions, but that genial gentleman merely laughed in reply.

"Forgive me, Lady Corby and Miss Corby," he said, as though he were the one at fault. "But Tony knows that it is not I who make the guest list. My dear wife takes care of all that, and with Allen to carve my joint for me, I am well cared for. Let me say that I sincerely hope you will come again to see us and that next time it will be for dinner, as well."

They bid him goodbye with sincere gratitude for his kindness to them and turned their steps homeward. The carriage was brought round, and Tony handed the ladies in, first Lady Corby and then Sophie. As their hands touched, Sophie was aware that she was still shaken by the feelings that had been aroused but a few minutes before. Tony's eyes met hers unsmilingly as he helped her into her seat, but she fancied he was having as much difficulty swallowing as she was herself.

There was not much opportunity for conversation on the way home. Once, Lady Corby referred aloud to her surprise at the rather regal way in which Lady Holland ordered the affairs of her household, and Tony responded thusly, "Do not be amazed at it, Lady Corby. All of Lord Holland's friends know that she must do just as she does. If she did not, their house would be filled with more guests than they could feed every night of the week. Lord Holland's congeniality knows no limits. But he is very happy."

Lady Corby smiled in understanding as she turned to Sophie. "Well, he certainly is a most cordial host. We had a lovely time, did we not, Sophie?"

Sophie could only smile and nod her head, but her smile held a certain dreaminess that made her mother refrain from further questions for the remainder of their trip home.

CHAPTER TEN

SOPHIE AWOKE THE NEXT MORNING and stretched with a delicious feeling of anticipation. Her dreams the previous night had been sweetened by the memory of Tony's scent and feel as he had leaned forward to kiss her under the arcades of Holland House. And her mind now was occupied with the pleasurable question of when and where that kiss would finally be consummated.

It had been weeks now since she had begun to think him the most handsome man of her acquaintance. The kindness and the laughter behind those clear blue eyes were surely what made him so attractive to her—and to everyone, she had no doubt. That he should interest himself in her was the only puzzle to Sophie, though she hoped he knew that in her he would find a partner quite willing to make him as happy as he so easily made her.

She got out of bed and prepared for the day, certain of its bringing her a delightful surprise and having no doubts that Tony would call. With a quickness to her movements that was totally unlike her, she dressed, paying special attention to the details of her toilet and directing the maid to select her most becoming morning gown. And as she dressed, she dreamed, though not in the vague, almost detached manner of the old Sophie, but with a lightness of heart that put a purpose in every move.

Downstairs, Sir John and Lady Corby were finishing their breakfast as their daughter arrived, her brown curls arranged becomingly about her face. Sir John had been telling Lady Corby about his successful expedition to Tattersall's with the impressive news that his friend had paid one thousand Guineas for the hunter at his urging, knowing the horse to be a rare gem. As Sophie joined them, he had just finished the story, and her entry reminded him of the benevolent interest he had shown in their activities of the previous day. And with a sense of everything being right with the world, he greeted her with unaccustomed approval.

"You are looking fine this morning, Sophie. Your outing seems to have put colour in your cheeks."

Sophie responded to his friendly overture with an even brighter glow. "Thank you, Papa. It was truly a wonderful day. Did Mama tell you that my poem was very kindly received at Holland House?"

She heard a strangling sound and looked up from her plate to find Sir John in a state approaching apoplexy. His face was purple, and the veins in his eyes were bulging. Her first thought was that he had choked upon a bite of food, but soon she realized that no blockage of air could produce the roar that came out of his mouth.

"Holland House! By God, Clarissa! What have you been about? You did not tell me you had been to Holland House!"

Lady Corby had turned white with fear, and Sophie knew suddenly that her mother had been trying to conceal the truth from him without asking for Sophie's complicity.

"Did I not, John?" said Lady Corby with a weak attempt at innocence. "I am terribly sorry, but I had no idea that you would disapprove."

"Disapprove!" roared Sir John. "Of course, I disapprove. Who took you there? How did you come to be invited? Certainly no one who calls himself a friend to John Corby would have taken you there."

Lady Corby avoided a direct answer, but Sophie, with a sinking heart, realized that the truth would soon come. "I take full responsibility for it, Sir John," her mother answered, "although I wonder at your degree of displeasure." Her tone begged an explanation of his anger, but Sophie was not deceived. Her mother had obviously feared Sir John's anger all along and had chosen simply not to heed it.

"You wonder?" Her father was almost speechless with incredulity. "You have entered the house of a divorced woman, taking our daughter with you, and you wonder at my displeasure?"

"But surely, my dear," Lady Corby said, defending herself boldly, "it cannot be thought so very wrong if so many of the best people do the same. The Prince Regent was known to dine there in earlier years, and Lady Jersey herself does not disdain to call." Her tone clearly implied which of the two was the more important visitor.

"But they are Whigs!" Sir John protested. "And I have heard it said in reliable circles that the Hollands sympathize with Bonaparte! Why they are little better than traitors to the Crown." Lady Corby declined responding to these charges, knowing the sentiment to be justified to a certain extent, but Sir John took her silence as a protest.

"And if that were not enough," he added in portentous tones, giving the final argument, "that woman ran out on Sir Godfrey Webster, a gentleman with whom I often rode in the field." His tone implied the heresy of such a betrayal.

Lady Corby gathered her courage once more to dispute his final reason. "But, John, dear, everyone said that Sir Godfrey abused her terribly and spent all her fortune on his stud."

"Nonsense," he muttered with a growl.

"And she was married to him at the age of sixteen. He must have married her for her fortune," she persisted, "which I understand he kept after the settlement."

"That is neither here nor there," Sir John said uncomfortably. "You are diverging from the issue. Who took you there?" he asked again, rallying on the attack.

Lady Corby remained silent, but an involuntary flicker of her eyes in Sophie's direction, revealed all he wanted to know.

"Farnham, was it?" he said, raising his voice again. "I should have known. The fellow's nothing better than a blue-coat! It's no wonder he refuses to hunt when he'd have to sport a Whig's colour." He shook his head with the enormity of the offence.

Sophie listened with growing dismay. Her innocent revelation had destroyed her hopes for a delightful day and now signalled trouble ahead. She knew that her father did not look favourably upon Tony, but she had assumed that his anxiety to see her settled before the cubbing season began would outweigh any aversion he might have towards him. Now she wondered if she should have taken his objections more seriously. There was nothing she could or would do to make Tony more acceptable to her father, but she had counted on Sir John's indifference. Perhaps, she thought, if Mr. Rollo were not so strongly to his liking, her father would not be so adamant in his dislike of Tony.

A moment more and her worst fears were realized. Sir John had jumped with his customary impulsiveness to a drastic solution. "I will not allow it," he said, striking the table with an open hand. "My daughter is not to be led to consort with Bonapartists and thistle-whippers! From now on, there will be no more riding out with Sir Tony Farnham. He must not think that he can befoul Sophie's reputation with questionable associations. And I want his calls to be limited in future. He has been allowed too great a degree of familiarity in this house, and it shall stop." Sir John's voice admitted no discussion.

And he was given none. Both Sophie and Lady Corby knew him far too well to argue when he was in a temper. Trusting, however, that time and indifference would soon soften his determination, Lady Corby merely acquiesced for the present. But Sophie, no longer wishing her breakfast, finished her meal with difficulty. She was torn between a desire to see Tony immediately and fear that he would call while her father was in such a temper. Her fear was lessened, though, when Sir John took leave of them for his club, grave disapproval in his countenance.

"I am sorry, my dear," said Lady Corby, knowing when she saw the pain on Sophie's face that her daughter's heart had been touched for the first time. "But do not set too much store by it. Your father's anger is never very long lasting. By tomorrow he will have something else on his mind, and eventually he will not think of Sir Tony so harshly. It is only a matter of time."

Sophie smiled wanly. The question of time was not so small an issue to her now that every one of her senses longed to experience Tony. And, too, she worried that the time remaining to them in London would not be enough to resolve her father's aversion to him.

As a way to take their minds off the scene at breakfast, Lady Corby suggested a trip to the subscription library, a suggestion which normally Sophie would have welcomed. But not today, for today certainly she could expect a call from Tony. Still, she could not tell her mother that she must stay home to receive his call without inviting uncomfortable questions, nor could she dissemble. So she agreed. And she consoled herself with the thought that he would call again and perhaps be better received when Sir John had had time to cool off.

Sophie would have been greatly alarmed to learn, however, that Sir John returned to the house in Berkeley Square just after noon to pick up a copy of the sporting journal he had left behind that morning. Finding the ladies gone, he decided to sit down and peruse it again before returning it to his friend Bumley. And he was so occupied when the bell rang and Tony entered the room.

He walked in with an eagerness in his step that was checked as soon as he saw the parlour's only inhabitant. He had been thinking about the light that now brightened Sophie's eyes whenever he entered the room and how the pleasure of that sight was soon to be his. Sir John's scowl was not the welcome look Tony had hoped to find, but he adjusted his thoughts quickly and approached with his usual cordial manner, doing his best to ignore the scowl. Faced with Tony's pleasant smile, Sir John could do nothing but greet him, though he invested that greeting with as little warmth as possible.

"Farnham," he mumbled shortly, "'servant." He did not rise, hoping to discourage the caller from staying. In truth, Sir John, although wishing to forbid Tony the house, could not deliver such an edict to a fellow gentleman without a greater provocation than he had been given. He had trusted that his own outburst would be sufficient to alarm Lady Corby into doing his will for him. Such had always been his way. Now, with Tony looking in an amused fashion at the unwelcome scowl on his face, Sir John felt the weakness of his position and the impossibility of enforcing it without embarrassment to himself.

They sat for a moment in uneasy silence. Sir John still hoped to discourage Tony with his inhospitable manners, and Tony, although amused by Sir John's bad temper, found it a definite barrier to conversation. Finally, he enquired after the ladies and expressed the hope that they were not too fatigued after the outing of the prior day.

"Not at all," was Sir John's curt reply. The resentment in his growl conveyed a certain understanding to Tony, and his lips twitched irrepressibly. Correctly assessing Sir John's opinion of the outing, he judged it best not to press the subject. Unfortunately the alternative topic which suggested itself to him proved to be a grave error.

"And how is your friend, Mr. Rollo?" beamed Tony. Since yesterday he had begun to discount that gentleman's threat to his own happiness and this confidence was a stimulant to his impudence.

"Fine," said Sir John, still unwilling to be drawn into conversation. But as he reflected upon Mr. Rollo, silently observing his superiority to present company, a marvellous thought occurred to him. As a solution it was perfect, for with it he would accomplish two objects: he would remove Sir Tony from his daughter's attention and he would secure a place nearest to her for the admirable Rollo. A smile replaced his alarming glare. His countenance was soon transformed, and Tony raised an eyebrow in contemplation of the rapid change.

Within moments, Sir John was regarding Tony with a benevolent and sympathetic eye. The simplicity of the solution had cheered him so that the words *poor boy* were actually in his thoughts. Unfortunately, this gave his next words to Tony a truthful ring, which they might not have otherwise had.

"It is fortunate that you should mention Mr. Rollo while we find ourselves alone here together, Farnham, for there is something about him which I ought to mention."

"Oh?" enquired Tony politely, despite the fact that Sir John's words had caused the hairs on the back of his neck to rise inexplicably.

"Yes," said Sir John, settling back in his chair comfortably. There was no suggestion of guilt in his tone and, indeed, he felt none. What he was about to say would certainly be the true case in a matter of weeks, if not days.

"You may be aware that Mr. Rollo has been spending a great deal of time with us lately, Sir Tony," he said, developing his topic enjoyably.

"Yes, sir," agreed Tony, then added significantly, "as have I."

Sir John glanced over at him with a slight look of displeasure, but recalled himself in time to take advantage of Tony's reply.

"Precisely," he stated. "It is about that that I wish to speak to you." Sir John leaned forward in his chair with an air of confidentiality. Tony leaned to meet him, but his smile had lost its warmth.

"You have been kind to us all, Sir Tony," continued Sophie's father. "Most kind. And we are all in your debt. For that reason, I judge it best to let you in on a little secret." Tony remained silent. "Our daughter Sophia has formed a favourable impression of my friend Mr. Rollo, and he of her. It is not to be wondered at, of course. The boy has much in common with the family, after all. At any rate, they have come to an understanding. I do not suppose I need explain."

Tony had straightened in his chair. His expression held none of the amusement that Sir John had habitually found in it. Instead, his eyes bored directly into Sir John's own, searching for some relief there and finding none. "You need not explain," he agreed.

"Good," said Sir John. "Now, as you said, your visits here have been frequent, and I am concerned that there may have been some talk as a result. And although we have not made an announcement yet, I am certain that neither you nor Sophia would wish for that to be the case. So I am suggesting, only suggesting, mind, that your calls be curtailed for the present. I hope I need not add that your absence will be felt by us all, but regard it only as a temporary condition. Once Sophia has established herself comfortably, well, then, naturally Lady Corby and I shall be happy to see you at any time in Leicestershire." He finished his speech with a convincing warmth, knowing that the likelihood of Tony's traveling so far on such a thankless errand would be improbable.

Tony stared at Sophie's father a moment longer. He was aware that Sir John had derived an enormous pleasure from making his announcement, but he could not doubt its truth all the same. Surely, Sir John would not invent such a story. And suddenly he thought he understood the meaning of Sophie's silence when he had asked her about marriage. Had she been going to kiss him? He would never know. Perhaps he had only imagined the dreamy submission he thought he had seen in her eyes. Aware of Sir John's watchful gaze upon him, Tony rose to his feet. The lightness was gone from his movements, but he managed to bow with a tolerable grace.

Not willing to discuss the matter with one whom he knew to be the engineer of his disappointment, however, he merely said, "You will be kind enough, I hope, to give Miss Corby my sincere wishes for her future happiness. And to you, my congratulations, Sir John." It was handsomely said, but not without special meaning. Sir John, however, felt only the truth of it. "Your servant," said Tony as he quitted the room and the house, never expecting to return.

Sir John chuckled joyfully over his success and took the liberty of enjoying a cheroot in the parlour while he finished his paper. By the time Sophie and her mother returned, he had left again for his club.

Lady Corby wondered, as they strolled in, if she did not detect a smell of smoke in the parlour, but Sophie was oblivious to it. She had immediately gone to the tray in the corridor to see if any cards had been left and had been puzzled, but a bit relieved, not to find any. Thinking only that Tony had not yet found the time to come around, she could only be grateful that she had not missed his call.

But the day passed, and there was still no sign of him. On the next day, Sophie pleaded a headache and listened painfully for a rap upon the door, but the only callers that day were two elderly ladies who had been friends of her grandmother. By the third day, Sophie was in a panic, certain that something horrible had happened to Tony and that no one had known to send her word. She fought the urge to ask her mother to write a note to Lady Farnham, not wanting to risk incurring Sir John's displeasure again by doing so.

Finally, as the week ended, Sophie came to the conclusion that her father had managed to waylay Tony outside his club and to deliver his edict. But she dared not ask him. His uncertain temper was always a deterrent to confrontation, and she knew that she would not be served by questioning him. She could only wait until the following Wednesday when she would surely see Tony at the assembly at Almack's, and she doubted that her father had gone so far as to forbid Tony to address her.

But on Wednesday she suffered a greater blow, for not only did she not have the chance to speak to Tony, she could not see that he was even present. She looked about the room throughout the evening, but never saw him, and she was reasonably certain that her eyes would have been drawn to him instinctively had he been there. Her partners could not help but notice that her interest was engaged elsewhere, and she was so lacking in spirits, in spite of her efforts to hide it, that none of them requested a second dance. For the first time since her appearance at the assembly room, she was obliged to sit out two of the dances. And that insult, added to her misery, only served to make her feel worse.

It was with a feeling of hopeless resignation that Sophie endured the next two weeks. Sir John saw to it that Mr. Rollo was a frequent guest to dinner. But learning from the lessons Tony had given her, Sophie was able to deflect his attention from herself at will by asking him about one of the hunts. Then she needed only to sit back and watch as Sir John and Mr. Rollo pursued the subject. Yet her father's ambitions on her behalf came closer and closer to being realized.

Rollo himself had not been reciprocal in the number of invitations he had made them. Aside from a few more rides in the park, to which Sophie only consented from the hopes of seeing Tony, and the "shilling well spent" at the Royal Academy, he had been most frugal in his entertaining of the Corbys. A man less inclined to favour him than Sir John might have been a bit suspicious of this lack of hospitality, but Sophie's father chose not to regard it, having in his own mind the urgent necessity of returning to Leicestershire in early June. To his way of thinking, all was going swimmingly, although he trusted Mr. Rollo would not disappoint him by ignoring the hunting calendar in choosing when to make his proposal.

At the end of the two weeks, however, Mr. Rollo was feeling the need to make a more costly bid for Miss Corby's hand and Sir John's heart. He made a trip to the city, and managed upon the credit of his failing

aunt, to borrow enough to fund a dinner party and a
night at Drury Lane. Sir John, not knowing, of course,
that his advice had been thus firmly ignored, accepted
the invitation for them all with the assurance of a
transaction being nearly complete.

They were treated to an excellent dinner at the White
Hart by a jovial host. Mr. Rollo, confident for once of
having a fat purse for the evening, did not refuse to
enjoy the claret himself. After dinner, they made their
way to Drury Lane in Mr. Rollo's own coach, and the
two gentlemen conversed pleasurably about the team
of horses. Sophie was silent, her mother noticed, as she
had been of late. There was no longer any colour about
her cheeks, and her eyes had lost the sparkle of youth
which had gleamed brighter than ever since their coming to London. Nor had Lady Corby failed to notice
that Sir Tony was suddenly absent from all their
doings, and she would have felt the absence on her own
account had she not felt it so strongly on her daughter's.

The first play to be performed that evening was
Shakespeare's *Othello*, and in different circumstances
Sophie would have been beside herself with expected
pleasure. But tonight, as she watched Edmund Kean
upon the stage, as thrilled as she was by his fine performance, she could only think of the time she had met
him as being the last day she had seen Tony. The play
threatened to move her beyond what was normal, and
she had to strive to maintain her sense of detachment.

At its end, however, she stood with the rest of the roaring crowd to applaud a flawless performance, wishing only that Mr. Kean could somehow meet her eye and convey to her with a look his knowledge of Tony's whereabouts.

The next play was to be a farce, but there was time in between for the audience to mix and to drift back and forth between the boxes. Again Sophie's father spared her from speaking to Mr. Rollo beyond thanking him for the rare treat, for he was as eager as ever to talk over old hunting days. Looking about the theatre, lost in thought and only half seeing the people around her, as had been her habit before meeting Tony, she suddenly came alert as she spied a well-loved figure across the balcony.

Tony had just entered one of the boxes and was now speaking to a lovely woman who was dressed in the height of fashion, *très décolleté*, her bosom decked with jewels. Sophie felt the anger rise within her as she remembered her fears for his safety and whereabouts, realizing that they had been nothing more than a substitution for the betrayal she should have felt. For Tony was perfectly well. Although she was observing him from a distance, she could see enough to know that the lady was flirting with him outrageously and that Tony's manner was not discouraging. Sophie watched as the lady, clearly not an ingenue, rapped him playfully with her fan, and she seethed as Tony leaned a bit closer to whisper in her ear. But she was not able to take her eyes off the scene, though every minute added to her torture.

The curtain went up for the farce to commence, and only then did Tony relinquish his seat by the pretty lady to the gentleman who had accompanied her. When he did, Sophie looked away quickly to avoid meeting his eyes should he chance to see her, not wanting him to know how badly she had been hurt. But presently, not able to stem her curiosity, she stole another glance. She fancied that he had been standing and staring fixedly at her, but as quickly as she had turned, so had he, and the last she saw of him was his back as he strode out of the box.

The result of this episode was that Sophie did not hear a word of the play that followed. Her heart was beating so strangely and so uncomfortably, that her mind could only race in errant circles. Earnestly did she hope that she would not encounter Sir Tony in the corridor as they left their box, and yet her eyes did not stop searching for him among the audience, despite the darkness of the theatre. Her heart was breaking, and the proof of it was the hurt that would not leave her chest.

The evening could not end too quickly for Sophie. Afterwards, she marvelled how she had found the strength to make her way outside the theatre, endure the long wait for their carriage and thank Mr. Rollo properly as he took them to their door. The ache within her seemed to affect her breathing strangely, yet she experienced it all as if in a dream and outwardly showed no sign of failing. It was not until she reached the comfort of her room later that she gave way to her emotions.

But before she could experience the relief of solitude, another worry was added to her agony. After telling his host good-night and accompanying the ladies indoors, Sir John requested their presence immediately in the parlour. Sophie would have pled a headache at this point had he not given an indication that what he had to say would be of particular importance to herself.

They entered the parlour, and Sir John took a moment to ring for a glass of port. Lady Corby and Sophie declined to join him with a glass of sherry, but they waited patiently for his to arrive before they asked for his news.

"Ah, yes," said Sir John, settling himself comfortably now that the servant had left the room. "I do have something to tell you that should interest you. Mr. Rollo, who has so kindly entertained us this evening, has just issued me a most interesting invitation." He glanced significantly over his goblet at Sophie. Her heart, which had seemed to throb with a dull ache, gave a lurch as she awaited his dreadful news. "He has," continued Sir John impressively, "asked me to accompany him to his estate on a fishing expedition. I do not need to tell you, Sophie, the significance I attach to his request.'' He took a sip of port and smiled at his ladies with satisfaction.

Lady Corby glanced rapidly at Sophie but could find no enthusiasm in her fixed regard. She did not doubt Sir John's interpretation of the event, for Mr. Rollo's attentions had always been particular and of late more so than ever. The evening to which he had just treated them had been attended by an air of celebration, the reason for which she did not have to search far. And now it seemed, Mr. Rollo wished to have some time alone with Sophie's father, when the subject of matrimony was certain to be discussed.

But Lady Corby had not failed to notice that Sophie had withdrawn of late. She had lost the gaiety and liveliness she had so lately acquired in Sir Tony's company and had seemed less in touch with her surroundings than ever before, even at home in Leicestershire. For this reason, her mother was reluctant to commit herself on the outcome of Mr. Rollo's suit. And although she foresaw dreadful possibilities if Sophie should refuse the young man, she intended to support her daughter whatever her wishes. So she responded in a more cautious tone than Sir John would have liked to hear.

''Indeed,'' she said noncommittally. ''That would seem to be most interesting. Mr. Rollo is certainly decided in his regard for you, Sir John,'' she added quite truthfully. Lady Corby encouraged her husband to expound upon the virtues of the young gentleman and kept her own responses cheerful until the warmth of his port could take his mind off the two young people. Then she quickly ushered Sophie off to bed before he could notice that she had not responded to his announcement.

CHAPTER ELEVEN

"I DON'T LIKE SOPHIE'S LOOKS," said Aunt Sadie a few days later as she sipped tea with Lady Corby in the parlour. "She looks all done up."

Lady Corby's eyes met those of her sister-in-law over the brim of her cup, which she then replaced carefully back on its saucer. "I know," she agreed, happy to have someone with whom to discuss Sophie's poor spirits. "I am afraid something has happened to distress her considerably, but she has not confided in me."

"It's not this Rollo fellow, is it?" enquired Sadie bluntly.

"Perhaps," said Lady Corby. "He is becoming very particular, you know. Still," she added, "I cannot help but think there might be another reason."

Sadie nodded her head wisely, but she was frowning with displeasure. "It's Tony, isn't it? He's hedged off."

Lady Corby shifted uncomfortably in her chair. Her sister-in-law's words were not the ones she would have chosen to use, but she did not intend to avoid addressing the issue. "I do not know. It seemed, at least for a while, that he was pursuing his interest with Sophie. I was almost certain . . ." She did not finish the thought. "Anyway, we have not seen him for some time now."

Sadie was still frowning deeply. "It doesn't figure, Clarissa. I would not have thought the boy could be so fickle. Sure, he is a bit hard to pin down at times, but I would have been willing to swear he was one you could count on. I don't like to be wrong about people," she said, ending on a threatening note.

"Let's not be hasty, Sadie," cautioned Lady Corby, not without some alarm. Then she chided herself for having entertained the thought, however briefly, that her sister-in-law meant to challenge Sir Tony to a duel. "We really do not know the facts in the case."

"Well," said her stout companion, "I do not like to see the gel getting thin and pale. Perhaps a drive would do her good. I remember her saying that she would like to learn to handle the reins, and there's nothing like a challenge to improve the spirits."

A few weeks ago, Lady Corby might not have agreed to the scheme so readily, but her concern for Sophie was now so strong that she was happy to accept any suggestion. So off she went in search of her daughter to persuade her at least to take the air in her aunt's phaeton. While she was absent from the room, Sir John came in from his club to take leave from the family before going on to Mr. Rollo's estate. He was hopeful of returning to London in a week's time with the terms of a marriage proposal all arranged.

Presently, Lady Corby and Sophie joined them, and Sir John, heartily approving the proposed outing, bade his daughter goodbye with the cheerful words, "I shall hope to have something to surprise you with, Sophie, when I get back to Town. And then," he added happily, "we may all be off for home and through with this nonsense."

"Papa," began Sophie with a touch of defeat in her voice. She had tried to make her feelings clear to him on a number of occasions since the night of the theatre party, but her strength had now been sapped by her own level of hopelessness. "I hope you do not mean to speak to Mr. Rollo of marriage, for I am certain that we would not suit."

In desperation, she had expressed herself more forcefully than ever before, and Sir John could not ignore her this time.

His collar threatened to strangle him as indignation took hold. "Nonsense, Sophie! Let us have no more on the matter! I have managed through diligence and hard planning to land a promising young man for you, one, moreover, whom I shall be delighted to call son-in-law, and you have the dashed ingratitude—I will try not to put it more forcefully—to threaten to decline his offer. Rollo can offer you a home, his estates and courage in the field that you can be proud of. Now, what more does a woman need? Your mother can tell you that that has been good enough for her all these years, and you will certainly not pretend to have better claims to happiness than she has. And," he added to his sister as she opened her mouth to speak, "I do not want to discuss it with *you*."

Her father's words about his own wife's happiness, Sophie reflected, were not as cheering as he had intended. But she declined to comment further. His mind was fixed and, short of a miracle, would not be changed. Her own mind was made up as well, and she had already decided on a plan of action if Mr. Rollo did, indeed, come up to scratch. She would refuse his offer, of course, no matter how much her father ranted and raved about it, and she doubted Sir John could force her to accept without sacrificing his own good name in the bargain. If he then cast her off (and she almost hoped that he would), she would apply to her Aunt Sadie for assistance, and she trusted that large-hearted lady would take her in. She had no doubt that they would deal well together, even if it meant for her retiring at an early age to the countryside in Kent.

Not wishing to debate the question further, Sir John kissed his sister and his wife goodbye and, declining to recognize Sophie with this sign of his affection, cautioned her to mind her manners until his return. Then he went off, muttering about ingratitude until the prospect of a country view offered him a happier subject for his thoughts.

"Well, Sophie," said Aunt Sadie, feeling, for once, powerless to offer much in the way of comfort, "let us go out for a turn to shake the cobwebs from our minds." She patted the girl almost gently on the back and received a grateful smile in return. Taking this for an answer, she led the way outside to where her carriage was waiting and spoke to the boy who was walking the horses.

"Get yourself up behind, Jemmy. Miss Corby will be joining me on the box." Her tiger held the horses' heads until the ladies were settled up in front and then ran quickly to jump on the back as the spirited team took a plunge. Sophie eyed them with a certain lack of confidence, but Aunt Sadie nodded her approval. "The leaders are still a bit frisky today," she said. "I'd rather that than a shirker. Now, watch me closely, Sophie, and listen to what I say." She headed them carefully out from the curb, but once they were out in traffic, allowed them to go at their own pace.

"You must place your feet firmly down on the footboards," she began, "to support you on the box. It would help," she added critically, "if you had more bottom, but perhaps it will come with age. Mine did." The reflection did not seem to dismay her.

As Sophie watched, Aunt Sadie gave her all the basic instructions she must have to begin to handle a team, and she listened with growing interest as the carriage raced at breakneck speed through the crowded city streets. A moment more, and they were at the gates to Hyde Park. Her aunt pulled the horses down to a trot as she prepared to hand her the reins. When they came to a stop, Sophie took the reins with a determination not to disgrace herself, although her heart beat unsteadily as she recalled their recent speed. Sadie helped to lace the ribbons through Sophie's fingers and promised to grab them if the horses threatened to run away.

With the intention of holding the horses to a walk if at all possible, Sophie gritted her teeth and "herrupped" the horses. Surprisingly, they obeyed her, which she credited to their more settled condition after the rapid trot from Berkeley Square.

"That's a gel," said Sadie approvingly. "I knew you could do it. Tap your leaders now and step it up to a trot. They won't try to run with you. That's it."

She kept up her encouraging remarks as Sophie circled the park a few times at a respectable pace. The clear air and the exercise were, indeed, having their effect, and Sophie was not so cast down that a challenge successfully met could not raise her spirits. As they reached the entrance to the park once again, she could be glad that she had agreed to the outing, for her improvement in spirits was helping to reconcile her to her impending fate. She could not help remembering, though, the first time she had driven in the park, and she was grateful to know that if she should spot Sir Tony driving there with his own team, she need not be ashamed of her own performance.

At this point, however, Sophie was ready to hand the ribbons back to her aunt, for a great deal of strength was required to hold the horses continuously in check, and she had not got the habit of it. Taking them then with more compliments on her niece's first efforts, Aunt Sadie led them back into the streets and in the direction of the city.

"I will take you to Crowther's, Sophie," she said, promising her a treat. "I am in need of a new coaching whip, and his is the only place where I would consider buying one. They're expensive, mind you. A guinea apiece. But they're the best there is."

She stepped up the pace as she headed out along Piccadilly past Bond Street, and Sophie, who was now forced to hold on to the box with both hands to maintain her seat, began to wish sincerely for more bottom. She wondered humourously at her mother's willingness to send her out for a ride with Aunt Sadie without providing a hartshorn in her reticule.

They arrived at Mr. Crowther's establishment and left the horses in Jemmy's able hands. Instantly upon entering, Sophie's nostrils were greeted with the rich smell of cured leather, and she found herself surrounded by thongs and whips of every description. There was a crowd of gentlemen near the back of the store, however, and Sadie suggested that Sophie leave to her the task of making her way through them to obtain Mr. Crowther's attention. Considering her aunt, whip in hand, to be ably armed for the task, Sophie began to walk about the crowded store, idly looking over the proprietor's craftsmanship.

The smell of the leather and the hum of conversation provided by the lounging amateur coachmen were all too familiar to Sophie, and before long she was wandering vaguely, little aware of her surroundings. Her thoughts were of Tony and the discovery she had just made that tanned leather was one of the faint elements of his own personal scent. But the shop was so strongly marked with the odour of leather that it had blotted out her sensual memory of Tony's nearness, and she strived to recapture it momentarily by closing her eyes. As she did so, however, she came to the end of a row of wares just as a gentleman rounded the corner, and she walked without check directly into his arms.

For one maddening, although embarrassed moment, Sophie thought that she had just managed to recapture the elusive memory of Tony's scent before accidentally running into the gentleman. Now with regret she would have to abandon her daydreams to deal with the present situation. But after taking a rapid step backward and looking up in order to apologize, she found that what she had done was to locate Tony himself.

She stared up at him in amazement and wondered dazedly if she had somehow acquired the scenting abilities of the famous Quorn hounds. From the expression on his face, she gathered that he was as surprised and disturbed by the encounter as she was herself. Although, despite the hurt he had dealt her, her heart quickened with the joy of seeing him again. They stood, gazing fixedly at one another, until presently something seemed to recall Tony to himself and he doffed his hat in polite greeting. The gesture, so elegantly made and so endearingly familiar, drew a faint, reminiscent smile from Sophie.

"Miss Corby," he said. "Your servant." His face was clouded with a distant look that seemed totally unlike the man she knew. He had called her Sophie the last time she had seen him, she recalled.

"How do you do, Sir Tony?" she asked, determined not to sound injured. "What a surprise to see you."

The corners of his mouth turned up in a wry smile, "I might say the same of you, Miss Corby, for I little suspected you to frequent Mr. Crowther's shop."

"No, of course not," she said, recollecting suddenly how odd her appearance there must seem. "I came only because of Aunt Sadie. She has been teaching me to drive her carriage, you see, and thought a trip to Mr. Crowther's would form a necessary part of the education."

"I see," he said, relaxing almost imperceptibly over something she had just said. "Your aunt is always correct on such matters." He hesitated for a moment and then said, replacing his beaver, "Please give her my warmest regards." He nodded and made as if to move away.

A feeling of panic entered Sophie's breast. When she had dreamed or thought of this encounter, she had never allowed herself to think that it would be concluded so quickly. The idea that she should yearn so deeply to speak to Tony again, and then, achieving a meeting, be cheated from receiving any comfort from it was more than she could bear. Her pride, which she had counted on to hold her up through a chance meeting, meant nothing to her now that his back was almost turned. So she called out in a note of desperation which bore the weight of her weeks of unhappiness.

"Sir Tony," she called. He turned almost cautiously.

"Yes, Miss Corby?"

She swallowed as her mind groped hopelessly for words. "We have missed seeing you in Berkeley Square, of late." As an excuse to resume speaking, perhaps, the words were rather weak, but they were delivered in such a peculiar way that Tony must have thought them worth attending. He stepped closer to her, as his eyes looked into hers searchingly.

"I have regretted being unable to call," was all he said. If Sophie had hoped for an explanation, it was not offered, but still Tony watched her as though any explanation should be hers instead. Her eyes wavered under his regard, and she waited tensely, expecting him at any second to depart again. But to her surprise, he offered this comment.

"May I take the liberty, Miss Corby, of wishing you joy in your impending union?"

His tone was all that was proper, but Sophie stared in astonishment as he came to an end.

"Impending union?" she exclaimed, wondering what he could possibly mean. "What union, Sir Tony?"

"Your intended marriage to Mr. Rollo, Miss Corby," he explained, with a look of frowning enquiry.

"But I have *no* such intentions with respect to that gentleman," she protested. Tony's eyes had not left her face, and he was now regarding her with a curious mixture of distrust and hope. She flushed unhappily. "Who, may I ask, is responsible for spreading such a malicious untruth?"

Tony's expression had brightened as rapidly as her outrage had mounted, and his lips twitched irrepressibly as he divulged his source.

"I'm afraid it was your father, Miss Corby."

Sophie blanched and then coloured with anger as she realized the extent of her father's interference. She hung her head while attempting to control her rare anger and, finally, responded with embarrassment. "My father is mistaken," she said uncomfortably.

Just then, her Aunt Sadie's voice boomed out from behind her, "There you are, Sophie." She stepped up behind her niece with an air of high frustration. "I shall have to keep you waiting another while..." she began, and then stopped as she perceived Tony with them. "Sir Tony!" she said with an accusatory frown. "So this is where you've been for the past few weeks." A lesser man would have been quelled by the displeasure in her regard.

But Tony laughed without reserve, and Sophie dimpled helplessly as she witnessed the restoration of his happy looks.

"I'm afraid it has all been an unfortunate misunderstanding, Miss Sadie," he explained, giving Sophie a look of deep contentment. Staring back and forth from one to the other of them, Aunt Sadie relaxed her stern expression.

"Good," she said, not troubling them to explain themselves. "Then it's fortunate we should run into you here. It seems that I shall be held up a few minutes more while the shopkeeper trims the thongs on my whip. I might suggest that you take Sophie out into the street for a stroll up and down while I keep the fellow's mind to his work. He's got too many customers today to stick with it if I'm not standing over him."

"Gladly," said Tony, offering his arm to Sophie with a smile that threatened to take her breath away. "We'll be waiting for you out in the street."

Sophie took his tendered arm with a shaking hand, overcome with the rapid change in the state of her emotions, and stepped gratefully out into the busy street. The fresher air outdoors eased the tightening of her chest, and she stole a look up at Tony, expecting not to be able to meet his direct gaze. But the happiness in her companion's eyes was like a magnet to her own, and she found, instead, that she was unable to turn away as the dimples burrowed deeply into her cheeks.

They had not begun to speak before they were assailed by an importunate street vendor who approached Sophie in the garb of a cleric.

"Pardon me, my lady," he said with the gravest possible dignity. "Permit me to h'offer you a copy of *The Last Dying Speech and Confession of Cadger Lummy*."

Sophie was momentarily disconcerted by the grimness of the subject, but said, "No, thank you," and would have passed on except that the vendor had placed himself in their path.

"Well, then, 'ow about the *h'Elegy for Chaffing Tom, the Mace King*," he persisted. "It was written by the Wretched Culprit 'imself, just before 'is h'execution."

"Ah, yes, Miss Corby," agreed Tony to her surprise, and still in the greatest good humour. "I must not let you pass up such a valuable acquisition. Do let me obtain one for you."

The vendor smiled graciously and offered Tony a flimsy pamphlet, which had been printed in chipped type and decorated with crude woodcuts. "H'a special price for you, sir, just two pennies," he said.

"A duce instead of a win?" asked Tony, not at all displeased by the vendor's attempt to cheat him. "No thank you, my good man, they usually sell for one." The cleric acknowledged his customer's superior knowledge and accepted the single penny.

Throughout this exchange, Sophie had stared at Tony with an expression which was at once amused and puzzled and, seeing it now, he explained. "You think I belong in Bedlam, don't you, Miss Corby? I can see it in your eyes. But you do not realize the chance that you were about to throw away here. And as a fellow poet, I could not let you pass up this opportunity to obtain a copy of one of the representative works of our time."

Sophie still smiled sceptically, but the vendor, who had heard it all, beamed with pride and expressed his gratification with a deep bow. "Sir," he said. "H'I am h'onoured."

"Pitts Press, is it?" asked Tony, thumbing through the thin pages.

"Catnach," corrected the vendor.

"Of course," agreed Tony. "And if I am not mistaken," he added, favouring the cleric with a nod of recognition, "we are in the presence of the author."

The little man's sense of pride was so deeply gratified that it caused him to squirm with pleasure and threatened to overcome his carefully acquired dignity. "H'I cannot deny it, sir," he said. "But," he said, realizing that he had sold the work as a true confession, "h'I h'attended the Culprit as 'e h'ascended the gallows, miss, and h'I was Witness to 'is Wretched Penitence."

"Capital! An excellent way to make a shilling," said Tony, and Sophie, understanding him now, listened with delight.

"Listen to this, Sophie," began Tony. "The prose fairly oozes with penitence. 'Oh, harken to my Sorrowful Lamentation.' That's good. Or this, 'Please ask the Lord to spare my mother's tears.' Do you realize," he asked, smiling down into her upturned face, "just how much talent is required to create a poem from what this scoundrel probably said? If he mentioned his mother at all, it was more to the tune of (changing his voice to a low growl), 'tell me mum not to nap 'er bib.'" Sophie giggled. "But I suspect," Tony concluded, "he only bewailed the fact that he had been 'lagged by the traps for the rum ken he bumbled.' Am I right?" he said, turning to the street vendor for confirmation.

"H'indeed, yes, sir," agreed the man, happy to have a customer who understood his labours so well. But he beat a hasty retreat as Aunt Sadie, done with her errand and armed with a new coach whip, bore down upon him with her whip handle threatening.

"Be off with you, you mangy dog," she said, clearing him from the pathway with a few vicious jabs. "I'm surprised at you, Tony, for letting that fellow intrude upon you and Sophie. You might get lice. Should have sent him about his business," she added stoutly.

"Yes, ma'am," said Tony meekly, but he smuggled the pamphlet into Sophie's hand with a conspiratorial glance, which she answered with another giggle.

Sadie looked from one to the other of them non-plussed, but she soon sobered them by saying, "We'd best be going."

Sophie's smile faded rapidly, and her clutch on Tony's arm tightened involuntarily as if she feared not to see him again. He gave her hand a reassuring squeeze, but addressed his remarks to Aunt Sadie.

"There is to be a masquerade tomorrow evening at the Opera. Do you go?"

"It's not very likely," said Sadie with a huff. "Can you see me dressed as a dairy maid? And I doubt Sophie's mother would like it."

"But you must," exclaimed Tony with, Sophie thought, well-feigned incredulity. "All the Ton will be there. I can vouch for it personally."

"You can, can you?" said Sadie, not uncharmed by his persuasion. "Well, we'll see what we can do about it."

Tony thanked her sincerely and turned to take his leave of Sophie saying, "You will not want to make a habit of attending masquerades, Miss Corby, I know. But it is something that everyone should experience at least once—and preferably tomorrow night. And," he added provocatively as he bowed low over her hand, his gaze firmly fixed on her face, "at a masquerade one may do things that one would never do unmasked." The message Sophie read in his eyes caused her to tremble deliciously from her head to her toes, but she answered him shyly with a nod and a dimple.

Tony accompanied them back to their carriage and helped Sophie in before turning to Aunt Sadie and asking in a whisper, "How shall I know you?"

"Impudent rascal," said Sadie, tapping him playfully on the chest. "I can't tell you what we'll be wearing for I don't know yet, but you can look for me to be in something long and flowing. That should limit you, for I expect half the damsels there will be in shocking states of undress. I don't know what you're up to, but I trust you won't disappoint me." She gave him a keen look.

"You may have full faith and confidence in me, my lady," said Tony impishly, but Sadie did not doubt his words. With a satisfied nod, she allowed him to assist her up onto the box, and touching the leader's shoulder lightly with her new whip, off she drove.

CHAPTER TWELVE

LADY CORBY WAS NOT at all certain that a masquerade was the thing for a young lady to attend, but she was assured by Sadie that on occasion it could be allowed. She applied to one or two friends for confirmation and found that there was general agreement that if a girl were properly chaperoned, no harm would come to her, and there was the added advantage that in costume one was certain of not being recognized. Added to these reassurances was the pleading of her own daughter, who had been miraculously restored to joyous spirits after the experience of one day's outing. So Lady Corby found herself consenting to another scheme, of which, she was sure, Sir John would disapprove. At the very least, she told herself privately, Sophie's chaperon would be the least likely to be imposed upon in the crowd.

The day of the masquerade was entirely occupied in the hurry of finding a costume to wear in the evening. The tradesmen were applied to at this rather late date, but Sophie was easily fitted into the garb of a shepherdess, whose simple white blouse, apron and skirt suited her lovely, youthful figure to perfection. The skirt was shorter than she was accustomed to wearing, so a pair of neat stockings were added to clothe her legs below the knee.

But the sight of Aunt Sadie in her costume provided something of a shock, for she arrived that evening in the habit of a nun.

"You needn't look so scandalized, Clarissa," said Sadie, colouring a little, "I am not in want of taste. But there were no other costumes to be had which would cover my bulky figure. It seems that masqueraders try to *uncover* as much as they ordinarily cover to make up for the addition of a mask, but I would much rather be pegged for sacrilege than a show of indecency. I shall leave the rest to your imagination. Come along, Sophie," she finished, taking her niece by the arm, and the oddly-dressed couple made their way to the Opera in the company of a footman.

As Sophie entered the Opera House a half-hour later, she had to stop and stare in amazement at the scene before her. It was some time before her mind could take in the variety of the spectacle, both above, where the boxes were filled by ladies and gentlemen in differing degrees of costume, and below, where the revellers were engaged in all sorts of alarming behaviour.

The persons who had chosen to dress in their customary evening habits were disguised by hand-held masks, some in hats as well, and the décolleté of the

ladies was noticeable in its extreme. Some wore domi-
noes, but by far the majority were dressed as recogni-
zable characters. The stage was hidden by the large
number of people in front of it, who were principally
engaged in dancing, but the stage scenery of an Italian
city provided a romantic backdrop. Light shone from
the enormous chandeliers above, and someone, presumably a stage actor, was hanging by the waist from
a rope which stretched from one corner of the ceiling
to another. He gave the appearance of a tight-rope
walker.

But the dancers below provided Sophie the greatest
opportunity for observation, for she had never seen
ladies and gentlemen engaged in such riotous behaviour. One man, dressed in a cat costume, was down on
his knees before a country maiden, nuzzling her gown
in the most shocking manner. Another lady, dressed as
an Olympian goddess, was jumping rope in the middle
of the room beside an amused Zeus, and a milkmaid
was dancing with a Spanish conquistador while holding a milk stool in her hand.

The sight of all these things was overpowering, as
was the degree of familiarity exhibited between the men
and women present. Sophie's eyes widened in fascination as she watched an elegantly dressed young man,
himself completely free of masquerade, approach a
woman in the garb of a nun and wrap his arm around
her waist. And the nun's response was even more

shocking, for she showed no inclination to object to this arrogant affront.

Sophie averted her gaze from what succeeded and began to scan the room in the hope of finding Tony. But her heart sank as she realized the impossibility of identifying him amid the crowd. She had never known how successfully a mask, and especially a full-dress costume, could conceal a person's identity, and she could now see why licentious behaviour would run no risk of public censure.

As she waited there for something to occur, a flicker of doubt crossed her mind. What if Tony had not come? What if he did not find her? Or worse, what if she had completely misread the events of the previous day? Surely she had not mistaken the significance of the change in his demeanour, from the stiff distance with which he had first greeted her to the unalloyed joy when he discovered that she was not engaged to Mr. Rollo. Nothing had been spoken, but so much had been understood—or so it had seemed. Sophie had come to the masquerade with the certainty that tonight Tony meant to finish the kiss which they had almost exchanged at Holland House, and this time, she did not mean to resist.

As her mind dwelt on these thoughts, she was approached by a gentleman in a black domino who might possibly be Tony. He was about the right height and weight, although in the confusing light, where even the colour of his eyes was not clear to her, she wondered if memory was serving her right. He bowed low, politely asking Aunt Sadie for the privilege of taking her charge out onto the floor, and Sadie, thinking, too, that it was Tony, agreed.

Sophie gave him her hand and was reassured by the friendly squeeze he gave it, but once out on the floor, her confidence wavered when she detected the odour of spirits on his breath. And the dance, she suddenly realized, being a waltz, brought the man in the black domino closer to her than any gentleman had been in her life.

Her partner clasped her tightly around the waist with a quickness that almost frightened her. Her head was all confusion. But, in spite of the confusion, the sparkling lights and the whirling of the room around her, she began to know instinctively that the man who held her so tightly was not Tony. There was no familiarity to his scent, no comfort in his touch and no pleasurable excitement as his eyes travelled over her in silent appreciation. And the conviction that he was *not* Tony grew rapidly as the urgent need to escape his clutches increased. For after one quick turn about the room, the man in the black domino stopped dancing and started to propose other plans for the evening.

"Your pardon," said a man's voice beside them, as Sophie tried to extract herself from the domino's embrace. Her partner, so addressed, turned to see who had spoken and found himself confronted by a huntsman in a coat and mask of forest green. He was carrying a long whip, which he held stretched between his two hands, and his hold on the whip's handle was so tight that his knuckles showed white beneath his skin.

"May I make the suggestion, Sir Domino," he said politely, "that you find another partner for the remainder of the dance."

The black domino laughed uncertainly in his drunkenness, not at all certain how to respond to such an unusual suggestion. "You may," he answered with a touch of insolence, "but I am happy with the partner I now have."

"Of course, you are," said the huntsman with a gallant bow in Sophie's direction. "But I think you will soon find that you have mistaken your shepherdess." His tone held a note of special meaning, which Sophie could not decipher, but her heart gave a leap as she thought she recognized the voice behind the huntsman's mask. She looked at him more closely, but cautiously, determined not to make the same mistake twice.

The black domino was shaking his head stubbornly. "There's no mistake," he said with conviction. "She came in with the abbess."

"But not *the* abbess," persisted the huntsman. "And besides," he said pleasantly, trying to change his tack since the first proved to have no effect on the drunken domino, "T'was I gave the view-halloo."

Sophie looked at the newcomer hopefully as a grin accompanied these words, but the effect on her part-

ner was not a happy one. Seizing her suddenly around
the waist with one arm, he laughed and replied, "Oh,
a vixen, is she? So that is why you want her for yourself."

But Sophie had no chance to respond to the unpleasantness of his remarks, for more quickly than she
could react, the huntsman's whip had lashed out from
his right hand and caught the black domino around the
legs. And a blow to the jaw from the huntsman's left
hand quickly followed. The black domino, with one
motion, released her and crumpled to the floor. Someone cried out, and a woman screamed, but the huntsman showed no signs of alarm.

"I'm afraid he's tripped over my whip," he said regretfully, "and likely bumped his head." He mo-
tioned to two servants who had hastened toward the
commotion. "Perhaps he will feel more the thing after
a rest in one of the boxes," he suggested helpfully, as
they stooped to pick up the injured man. Sophie had
watched in fascination, shaken by the rapidity of
events, her hand up to her lips to stifle a cry as the
domino had fallen beside her. Now, she gazed at the
huntsman uncertainly, not knowing what to do. Surely,
she thought, she could not be mistaken in the easy
grace with which her rescuer had disposed of his rival.

The huntsman stood and faced her in silence until
the black domino had been helped from the floor and
the dancers had gone back to their own occupations.
Then he extended his hands, and as she hesitated, said

softly, "Sophie?" A quick step later, and Sophie found herself wrapped tightly in the comfort of his arms. She clung to him gratefully while he stroked her hair until the shaky feeling subsided and was replaced by the awareness of his being so near. Reluctantly, she pulled away, but when she looked up, was greeted by the familiar twinkle in the blue of Tony's eyes.

"I'm so sorry," he said in explanation. "There were two abbesses here tonight and one of them was definitely not respectable. By the time I had determined the sort of disguise your Aunt Sadie was likely to wear, you had been claimed by the black domino, and I very nearly made the same mistake he did." He gazed at her intently, and something about his look caused her knees to weaken beneath her. He stretched out his hands, more slowly this time, to draw her to the dance, and she found herself once again moving into the fold of his arms. Her body merged perfectly with his as they swirled to the rhythm of the music, and though he held her in an embrace that was tender, they circled the room as one.

Dazed by the strength of new emotions, Sophie allowed herself to melt into the cradle of Tony's arms, to feel the strength of steel beneath his clothes and the warmth of his breath as he whispered against her hair. His words reached her through a mist of intoxication as he asked in husky tones, "Sophie, do you love me?"

Still in a dreamlike whirl, she raised her face invitingly and whispered back, "Yes."

The huntsman's eyes bore into hers from behind his mask, and she could feel the rapid beating of his heart as he held her closely to his chest. "Do you remember what I said to you before, my love," he asked tantalizingly, "that at a masquerade one may do what one might not otherwise do?"

Sophie's mind was a mass of confusion; she answered him dumbly with a nod. His face came close to hers as he whispered, "Then I shall take the kiss you owe me." She did not turn away, but lifted her face to welcome his embrace. And finally, his lips met hers, and she gave herself up to a tide of emotion that threatened to sweep her away.

But before the tide could consume them both, Tony put her gently away from him with a shaky laugh and started to speak. Then, thinking better of it, he drew her to him more roughly and clasped her tightly to his chest. He was about to kiss her again when suddenly they were ripped apart by a powerful grasp.

"Release my niece, you impudent scoundrel!" cried Aunt Sadie as she pulled Sophie out of Tony's reach. In her nun's habit, she made an awesome picture of righteous defence of the faith. Sophie started to protest, but was warned by a slight hand gesture from the huntsman to keep her peace. At a safe distance now from the outraged abbess, he merely bowed with a great show of respect, touched his hand to his cap and backed away from them until he was lost in the crowd.

Watching him go, but seeing a clear promise in his eyes, Sophie felt herself floating as if in a blissful languor. And yet, this languid state was far removed from the lethargy she had experienced over the previous few weeks. All her senses were tingling with wakefulness at the memory of Tony's touch. And just below her peaceful feeling of security, her mind and body were thrilled with the excitement of life and delight in the future. She was unable to take her eyes from the place where he had disappeared into the crowd of dancers, but Aunt Sadie was not similarly affected.

"Insolent beggars!" she was saying in disgusted tones. "We must leave here at once, Sophie. I have never been exposed to such a vulgar lot—the most improper suggestions have been made to me tonight! You can have no conception! I thought I had you well placed in Sir Tony's care, but I would not have taken my eyes off you if I had not been instantly surrounded by the most impudent . . . !" Sadie was too offended to finish her speech. "Anyway," she continued, trying to turn her mind from it, "I shall have a thing or two to say to Sir Tony about leaving you to the mercies of that blackguard. He should have known better than to release you to anyone but me."

"But the black domino was not Sir Tony," said Sophie, recalling her first partner with difficulty. She allowed Aunt Sadie to drag her from the room by one arm and followed her meekly outside and to their carriage. She did not want to disturb the pleasant haze which surrounded her by entering further into the conversation, but she thought Sadie should be clear on that one point at least. Fortunately, her aunt was in a state of such high dudgeon that Sophie did not need to add any more. Accepting the notion that the black domino was not Tony, Sadie continued to berate the masqueraders until she had Sophie safely home and put to bed.

CHAPTER THIRTEEN

LADY CORBY GLANCED UP from her stitching to steal a look at her daughter. It was the morning after the masquerade and Sophie had yet to comment upon the evening. Aunt Sadie, who was seated with them in the parlour, had already had much to say about the failure of the scheme, though she had not been so indiscreet as to relate the worst of their affronts. But Sophie had, so far, been silent. She seemed lost in a dreamy vagueness which was at once deeper and less despondent than her normal wanderings. She had not appeared at breakfast, but had dressed with particular care and was now seated near them in a lovely gown of palest green. Lady Corby had had to call her name a time or two before getting a response to the simplest questions, and it was clear that Sophie's mind was not remotely on the work in her lap.

"You must not have stayed for very long, then, Sadie," said Lady Corby, noting the time that they were gone. "I had not expected to see you back at such an early hour. Had you any pleasant partners, Sophie?" she asked.

"Yes," said Sophie, dimpling secretively. She did not elaborate.

"A gentleman in a black domino," supplied Aunt Sadie. "Seemed polite." She looked at her niece curiously. "Are you certain he wasn't Sir Tony, Sophie?"

"Oh, yes," said Sophie languidly. Her eyes glazed over with a telltale dreamy stare. Lady Corby and Aunt Sadie exchanged puzzled glances and turned to her again, but before they could pursue the subject, Sir Tony was announced at the door.

It was the first time he had called upon them in weeks, and Lady Corby lifted her head with sudden surprise. She looked quickly to her daughter, who had instantly come awake, and then back to their visitor, whose gaze had eagerly found Sophie's before broadening to include them all. With a lightened heart she rose to greet him.

"Sir Tony," she said with scarcely restrained warmth. "How good it is to see you." With never failing politeness, he spoke a greeting to each of them and took a chair beside Aunt Sadie. For once, however, he seemed at a loss for conversation, and Lady Corby thought she detected a certain impatience in his bearing. His motions were not restful, and he avoided Sophie's gaze with visible effort. Concerned by the change in his manner, Lady Corby attempted to put him at ease.

"Sadie and Sophie attended the masquerade at the Opera last night," she said to start them off.

"Did you enjoy it?" Tony asked, allowing himself a quick glance at Sophie before turning back to Aunt Sadie.

"Yes," said Sophie bluntly and more forcefully than she had uttered the same to her mother. She was fully alert now, from the moment he had entered the room, but she could not know how the eager light in her eyes had disturbed his own tranquility. It seemed to Sophie that he was avoiding her, which she did not understand. Since the night before, she had been wrapped in a fog of sensuous awareness that was entirely new and confusing to her, and the sight of Tony had been enough to quicken her heart to an almost unbearable pace. Lost as she had been in a cloud of happy dreams, she had almost expected him to sweep her into his arms as he strode into the room. Her mother and her Aunt Sadie she saw as mere shadows between them.

But Aunt Sadie was answering Tony's question as if it had been meant for her, and indeed, Tony, after his quick glance at Sophie, seemed to be giving her his attention.

"A shocking business!" repeated Aunt Sadie for his benefit. "I have never been exposed to such insults. Although," she added justly, "I have reason to believe my choice of costume might have had something to do with *that*. But that does not excuse the behaviour that Sophie was subjected to," Sadie said, wagging a finger at Tony. "I thought I had safely entrusted her to a gentleman, but the next thing I knew, another rascal was forcing his attentions on her in the most improper fashion.''

"Oh, dear!" exclaimed Sophie's mother.

"Oh?" enquired Tony politely.

"Yes," said Sadie gruffly. "Fellow dressed as a huntsman. If John had been there, he would have called the fellow to account, but I managed to turn him off without too much bother and brought Sophie home directly." She looked at Tony accusingly. "We looked for you, Sir Tony, and did not find you."

Throughout the telling of last night's adventure, Tony had regarded Aunt Sadie with the most polite attentiveness, and now he assumed an expression of total innocence. Suddenly struck by his innocent demeanour, Sadie asked suspiciously, "Just how *were* you dressed last night?"

Sophie's heart took a leap as she waited for Tony to answer. Now, certainly, was the time for his declaration and an end to all her weeks of waiting. Sir John would not be pleased, but she thought she could count on her mother and Aunt Sadie to understand and support her. She smiled at him expectantly, but did not catch his eye, and the next words he uttered wiped the smile completely from her face.

"I'm very sorry," he said, "but I'm afraid something happened which prevented me from attending at all." He went on to apologize in the most contrite terms for misleading them about the masquerade and expressed his regrets that they had been discomfitted. But Sophie did not hear the rest. She was hurt, stunned, and felt herself drawing back into a cloud of confusion.

She stood up abruptly, suddenly unable to tolerate being in the room a moment longer. "Pardon me," she said mechanically and, without waiting for an answer, walked quickly from the room.

Tony leapt to his feet as the two ladies looked after her in dismay. He took one step towards Lady Corby's chair and addressed her rapidly, "May I go to her, please?" Lady Corby looked up. Her mind had been rattled by the speed with which things were happening, and although she suspected something had occurred to upset Sophie's heart with respect to Tony, she had not the slightest idea what it could have been. She started to protest, but her hand was quickly caught in his and Tony appealed to her with urgent entreaty. "Please," he said again quietly.

She searched his face for understanding and found something there which comforted her. "All right," she said with perfect composure, as though a young man chasing her daughter up the stairs would be nothing out of the ordinary.

Tony caught up with Sophie on the first landing, after ignoring the footman's offer for assistance in finding his way out. That respectable servant gazed on in fascination as the young lady of the house was enveloped in an amorous hug from behind.

"Sophie," said Tony softly as he kissed the back of her hair and neck. "What's wrong?"

He got no answer, but there was a noticeable relaxation of the stiffness in her back.

"Did I say something to offend you?" He tried to reach his head around to one cheek to feel for the appearance of a dimple, but she turned her face away in silence, apparently not appeased.

"Oh, Sophie," he said in a caressing tone, "didn't you know I gave the view-halloo when I first saw you?"

That speech did the trick, and Sophie whirled around in the fold of his arms to look at him accusingly. "So it *was* you, wasn't it?" she charged, at the same time allowing him to wrap his arms securely round her waist.

"Well, I should hope so," he said in a righteous tone.

"Then why did you lie?" she asked, still not satisfied with his answers. "I thought you said you were a truthful person."

"I am," said Tony blithely, "when the truth doesn't threaten my chances with my beloved." He paused, but when he saw she had not forgiven him yet, he added, "How should your mother have reacted if I had admitted being the 'scoundrel' who kissed you at the ball?"

Sophie buried her face in his shirtfront and clung tightly to the lapels of his coat. After trying unsuccessfully to work his face down closer to the vicinity of hers, he asked her pleadingly, "Please look up at me,

Sophie. Don't you know by now that I'm nutty about you?''

She peeked up at him from beneath thick lashes and allowed the first of two dimples to appear. "Does that mean what I think it does?"

"It does, Sophia *mia*. It is a cant expression for the fact that I am wildly in love with you. Now raise your head higher, please, so I can kiss you."

This time Sophie responded with full compliance, and the footman in the corridor so far forgot himself as to open his mouth wide and grin.

"There is one more thing I should tell you before your father comes home, darling," said Tony later, as he brushed his lips gently over Sophie's tempting cheeks. "And I'll confess to being the huntsman, too, after we are safely married, so you'll be convinced of how truthful I can be."

"Are we going to be married?" murmured Sophie in a blissful daze. "My father will not be pleased." She found it hard to express much alarm when all her senses were being so artfully aroused.

"He may come around when I let him in on a little secret," whispered Tony while nibbling her left ear.

"Oh?" mumbled Sophie. And then she started abruptly. "Oh, Tony. It's not about the Cyprians, is it?" she asked with wide-opened eyes.

"No," he said, chuckling delightedly. "It's not about the Cyprians, my love. You may forget all about them. But I will let you in on it if you promise to love me still."

"Yes?"

Tony drew close again and whispered softly in her ear, "I rather enjoy hunting."

"You do?" she cried, drawing back to face him indignantly. The Cyprians were clearly not in the same category of deceit. "But you said..."

"I know. That I don't hunt. And that's true. I decided long ago that it was too consuming a pastime and that I would not spend my life in one pursuit. But if it will make your father at all reconciled to our match—and you should not mind too much—I could hunt occasionally with him."

Sophie looked at him fearfully.

"I promise," he said, and she could not doubt his earnestness. "I shall not spend more than a few days a year in the field. We shall be much too busy doing things together in London to go often into Leicestershire."

Lady Corby opened the parlour door slightly and peeped round the corner of it in time to see Sophie throw her arms about Tony's neck and kiss him shamelessly. Withdrawing her head immediately, she thought for an instant, and then, deciding she had best leave things as they were, returned to her chair.

"Sophie all right?" asked Sadie anxiously.

"Yes, I think so," answered her sister-in-law calmly, but she was unable to conceal the little smile that followed her words.

"Humph!" said Sadie, raising one eyebrow, but it was a "humph" of pleasure.

Moments later, as Tony released Sophie with a sound of satisfaction, a carriage was heard pulling up in the street with Sir John's unmistakable voice roaring his instructions to the postboy. Raising her head in alarm, Sophie felt herself being drawn quickly out of sight of the front door, just an instant before it opened and her father's steps sounded in the corridor.

"It's Papa!" she whispered to Tony. "He was not supposed to be back from Mr. Rollo's for days!"

"Well, let's hope it's a bad sign for our friend Rollo," said Tony, continuing to nuzzle the base of her neck.

"Shouldn't you speak to him?" she asked, trying to keep from laughing as the outrageousness of Tony's behaviour occurred to her.

"I will," sighed Tony. "All in good time. But if I am about to be forbidden the house again—even just until your mother can talk him around—I would rather have something to remember you by."

Sophie dimpled and said nothing more.

Meanwhile, in the parlour, Sir John's unexpected return was causing something of a flurry. He plunked himself down in a chair amidst the ladies' startled exclamations and worried glances, but as he did not appear to be in a violent rage, they had to conclude that something had prevented his view of the stair landing. Breathing slightly easier as this thought came to her, Lady Corby began the questions.

"What happened, Sir John? Why are you here? We did not expect you home before Tuesday."

Her husband groaned wearily. He wiped his head with a handkerchief and leaned back in his chair as though exhausted with emotion. "I had to come back, Clarissa," he said. "I have never been so led on in my life."

"Led on, John?" the ladies prompted.

"Deceived," he answered heavily. "Never been so deceived in a man's character." His voice was weary with the profundity of his sadness.

Lady Corby threw Aunt Sadie a hopeful glance. "In Mr. Rollo, dear?" she asked incredulously.

He nodded. It was easy to see that the mention of his host's name was almost painful to him.

"Was it his estate?" asked Sadie bluntly. "Remember, I told you I'd heard he was all to pieces," she reminded him.

"No, not that," said Sir John, waving it aside impatiently. Then he added more judiciously, "Although I shouldn't wonder if you were right after all, Sadie. The man is capable of anything."

Lady Corby's eyes were dancing with delight, but she tried to keep a sympathetic expression as she said, "Tell us about it, John."

"All right," he said, heaving a great sigh. "The first night, everything was fine. Good dinner. Excellent claret. Nothing to complain of in the company or the conversation. It only shows how easily one can be fooled," he concluded sadly. Then he went on, reddening with displeasure. "It was yesterday morning when we set out to go fishing that the scoundrel revealed himself." He fumed silently for a moment.

"Yes, dear?"

Sir John paled as he remembered the moment of revelation. "The villain uses live bait!" he cried. "I tell you, Clarissa and Sadie, the sight unmanned me."

Lady Corby smothered a disloyal smile, but Aunt Sadie coloured in outrage. "The lousie cur!" she exclaimed sympathetically. "What did you do, John?"

"I hardly knew what to do, Sadie," he admitted. "The man was my host. But before the day was out, I knew I had to leave. I could hardly eat. And I told the fellow what I thought of him," he said stoutly. "I could never mount someone like that on one of my horses."

Sadie nodded her approval, but Sir John was still distressed.

"And now, all my efforts are for nothing. I hardly know how to face Sophie with the news. Months wasted kicking our heels here in London and no husband to show for it. She'll likely be disappointed."

"But surely, Sir John," Lady Corby reminded him. "If Mr. Rollo is capable of such unpleasantness, he would not have made a suitable husband for our daughter."

"No," he agreed, reluctantly. "I suppose not. But I do not want to spend another day here in Town. She will have to find someone near home."

"Oh, I think not, dear," said Lady Corby comfortingly. "I rather think Sir Tony could still be persuaded to marry Sophie. He really is such a nice gentleman."

"And an excellent whip!" added Sadie helpfully.

They waited anxiously for his response, but to both ladies' surprise, Sir John did not appear disgruntled by their suggestion. "Do you think so?" he asked pathetically.

They nodded.

"Well, better to make do with what's there," he said, accepting the inferior situation philosophically. "I shall have to get to work on him soon, though. Cubbing season's just around the corner."

He stared at the floor morosely, while his wife and sister exchanged pleased glances. Lady Corby allowed him to ponder for a while before trying to take his mind off his injuries, but presently she thought about their return home.

"Sir John," she said, "I've been thinking."

"What about, Clarissa?" he asked listlessly.

"I should like to take up something when we go back into Leicestershire. The children are getting older now and do not need so much of my attention."

"Take up something?" he asked, completely puzzled.

"Yes," she said smiling down at her work with quiet certainty. "Something like bees."